"What you do stinks, Brewer. You trade in wholesale death."

"It's a business that's been around a long time."

"That doesn't justify it," Mack Bolan growled. "Lately you've been handling stolen weapons, some from U.S. military bases. If you get picked up for that, my offer will start to sound real good."

"I'm too far gone for that 'death before dishonor' crap. The industrial nations are in the arms business up to their necks. Some of my best customers are government agencies."

"I don't play by government rules. If I decide you die, there's no vote on it."

Brewer shook his head. "How the hell do I walk away from this one? Every hard case in Holland wants me dead."

"Then do yourself a favor," the Executioner suggested. "Give me what I want and you can walk away."

"Okay. A boatyard upriver is home port to a sixty-foot cruiser called *Dark Runner*. It belongs to the Rotterdam syndicate. I'll draw you a map."

Moments later Bolan accepted the proffered piece of paper and headed for the door, saying, "You've earned a stay of execution."

"Dependant on what?"

"On whether you've told me the truth," the warrior stated with chilling finality.

MACK BOLAN ®

The Executioner

DON PENDLETON'S

EXECUTIONER
THE

HOSTILE ACTION

A GOLD EAGLE BOOK FROM
WORLDWIDE.

TORONTO • NEW YORK • LONDON
AMSTERDAM • PARIS • SYDNEY • HAMBURG
STOCKHOLM • ATHENS • TOKYO • MILAN
MADRID • WARSAW • BUDAPEST • AUCKLAND

First edition January 1995
ISBN 0-373-61193-5

Special thanks and acknowledgment to
Michael Linaker for his contribution to this work.

HOSTILE ACTION

Our sympathy is cold to the relation of distant misery.

—Edward Gibbon
1737-1794

Most decent folk will lend a helping hand to those in need. But there are others who seek to enslave even those who have nothing. They'll succeed over my dead body.

—Mack Bolan

THE
MACK BOLAN®
LEGEND

Nothing less than a war could have fashioned the destiny of the man called Mack Bolan. Bolan earned the Executioner title in the jungle hell of Vietnam.

But this soldier also wore another name—Sergeant Mercy. He was so tagged because of the compassion he showed to wounded comrades-in-arms and Vietnamese civilians.

Mack Bolan's second tour of duty ended prematurely when he was given emergency leave to return home and bury his family, victims of the Mob. Then he declared a one-man war against the Mafia.

He confronted the Families head-on from coast to coast, and soon a hope of victory began to appear. But Bolan had broken society's every rule. That same society started gunning for this elusive warrior—to no avail.

So Bolan was offered amnesty to work within the system against terrorism. This time, as an employee of Uncle Sam, Bolan became Colonel John Phoenix. With a command center at Stony Man Farm in Virginia, he and his new allies—Able Team and Phoenix Force—waged relentless war on a new adversary: the KGB.

But when his one true love, April Rose, died at the hands of the Soviet terror machine, Bolan severed all ties with Establishment authority.

Now, after a lengthy lone-wolf struggle and much soul-searching, the Executioner has agreed to enter an "arm's-length" alliance with his government once more, reserving the right to pursue personal missions in his Everlasting War.

1

The evening was chill, with rain slanting down out of a darkening sky. It was less than hospitable.

Mack Bolan, a.k.a. the Executioner, had been in Amsterdam for less than an hour, and already an unknown enemy was trying to kill him.

He didn't waste time analyzing the gunners' motives. He accepted what was going down and responded in kind.

The red-haired woman at his side, already startled by the burst of gunfire, had her senses jolted even more at the appearance of a gun in Bolan's fist.

He gave her no opportunity to ask questions, roughly pushing her to the ground and telling her to stay down. As she burrowed her face in the wet grass, she heard the muffled chug of the suppressed Beretta 93-R as Bolan triggered a 3-round burst.

A man cried out in pain, and a body thumped to the ground.

One down, Bolan thought, two to go.

More autofire rang out. Bullets rattled against the side of Bolan's rental car. Glass shattered. A front tire burst, dropping the car on the steel rim and putting the vehicle out of action.

Bolan crouch-walked to the rear of the rental and peered around the trunk.

He picked up the scrape of shoe leather on the loose gravel at the rear of the red Citroën the woman had arrived in, and the low murmur of a man's voice, angry at something, someone. Then the owner of the voice rushed into view, clutching an Uzi to his chest.

The Executioner gave him the opportunity to reach the midway point between the parked vehicles, then raised himself above the level of the trunk just long enough to stroke the Beretta's trigger. The trio of 9 mm tumblers caught the gunner in midstride, drilling into his chest and pushing him off balance. He took a long, seemingly slow nosedive to the ground. He hit hard, the impact stunning him. He lay facedown, making soft, scrabbling movements until his body shut down completely.

Waiting for no more than a few seconds, Bolan leaned out to check the area. He could see that the first guy he'd stopped lay on his back, arms thrown wide apart, legs stiff and straight.

The warrior spotted more movement on the front far side of the Citroën, a figure blurred by the cold rain sheeting in from the dark, cloudy sky over the city. He watched as the gunner tried to decide what to do next. Bolan held the Beretta two-handed, braced across the wet surface of the rental's trunk. He waited for an opening, needing the other man to move a few inches so he would have the clear shot he needed.

When the guy did move, he made the fatal mistake of raising his head above the Citroën's roofline. He was exposed for only a couple of seconds, but it was long enough.

Bolan angled the muzzle of the 93-R and stroked the trigger. The 3-round burst cored the gunner's skull, twisting him away from the Citroën and down onto the ground.

The Executioner was up and running. He sprinted across the gap between the parked cars, pausing only long enough to kick the first gunner's autopistol away from his outstretched hand. The guy looked to be out of action, but that didn't guarantee he was.

Sleeving the chill rain from his face as he approached the rear of the Citroën, the Executioner took a fast look at the second gunner.

He was on his stomach, facedown in a wide puddle with bloodstained rainwater lapping at his ears. The back of his skull had been messily opened by the exiting 9 mm slugs.

Bolan approached him slowly, telling himself he was being overcautious. This guy wasn't going to move ever again. Even so, he kept the 93-R on the corpse until he'd taken possession of the 9 mm Uzi lying close to the body.

He repeated the exercise with the hardman who had attempted to storm his position behind the rental car. He was dead, too. Bolan made a thorough search of all three bodies. None carried any other weapons, though all had extra magazines for their individual arms. Bolan took a couple of spare magazines. Other than the spare ammunition, the men were clean.

Bolan returned to the rental to find that his companion was still facedown on the ground.

"You can get up now," he told her.

Kelly McBride climbed to her feet, examined her damp clothing and attempted to brush the marks from her pants.

"What a mess," she complained.

"The meeting, or your clothes?" Bolan asked.

"Both," she replied, pushing her thick wet hair away from her angry face. "Are they all dead?"

Bolan nodded.

McBride's eyes bored into his. "Just what the hell is going on? Why did they want to kill us?"

"I'm not sure. I'll take an educated guess that it has something to do with the information Charlie Diel asked you to pass to me."

McBride, hands on her hips, stared at Bolan with unconcealed impatience.

"I'll have a few words for him, as well," she stormed. "What has he gotten me into?"

"Let's get away from here," Bolan suggested. "Then we can talk."

"Your car or mine?" she asked with a trace of sarcasm.

Bolan went to the rental, pulled his carryall from the trunk, dumped it in the back of the Citroën and opened the passenger door.

"You going to stand in the rain all night?" he asked.

McBride strode to the vehicle and got behind the wheel. She started the engine and rolled the car out of the empty lot and back to the street, where she stood on the brake.

"Where to?" she asked.

"Your choice. But make it somewhere we can talk without attracting too much attention. We stay well away from your place. Someone's gone to a lot of trouble keeping tabs on you, so your place is bound to be staked out."

"This is getting better by the minute. Now I'm a fugitive. Should I look out for a one-armed man with a grudge?"

A ghost of a smile tugged at the warrior's lips. If nothing else, this Kelly McBride had spirit. He realized why Diel had picked her as his courier.

She took off with a squeal of tires, spinning the wheel and taking them down the side street, away from the weed-choked building lot that could easily have become their grave.

McBride drove with the assurance of someone familiar with her surroundings. She negotiated Amsterdam's narrow streets and bridges with ease. The Citroën rolled over cobbled stretches wet with rain. Often they were running alongside the canals, the waters streaked with the city's lights and dappled by the rain that continued to fall.

Beside the woman, Mack Bolan studied the night through the rearview mirror, alert for a possible tail. The unknown enemy who had already made hostile moves knew McBride's car. If they had backup on the streets, the red Citroën would be easy to spot. Someone had good intel, because they had tagged the meet.

Too many possibilities, he decided.

The only way to play it was to deal with events as they occurred.

The sweeping windshield wiper caught Bolan's attention. He watched the heavy raindrops smacking against the glass, and he recalled seeing similar drops rolling down the window of his hotel room in London as he had picked up the telephone and heard Hal Brognola's gruff tones....

"I NEED YOU HELP, Striker, on something urgent."

"Go ahead."

"An agent in Amsterdam has some intel he needs to get through to D.C. He's been working undercover for a few months, gathering evidence of illegal arms dealing. A lot of the weapons involved have been coming from U.S. military sources here in the States and Europe. Three people have died during those thefts. He's been in Holland for the past few weeks. A week ago our man told Washington he'd picked up on something else. It was connected with the arms dealing, but liable to blow up into something bigger. He hinted at drugs being involved, as well. Two days ago he got a message through that his cover had been blown. Since then he's been on the run, trying to keep away from the opposition until he can pass his information to a friendly face.

"The word reached me at Stony Man, and I offered to pitch in. There's a flight being fixed for you out of Heathrow. I did some discreet string pulling to get you clearance, so some people will know Mike Belasko's in town. You'll have diplomatic immunity at both ends. Our consulate in Holland will have a rental car waiting for you at Schiphol Airport with all your 'luggage.' Our undercover man will pass you the goods without getting you spotted, then carry on and lead the opposition away so you can get clear.''

Bolan digested the briefing.

"Striker? Is there a problem?"

"Probably not. It just reads as being too easy."

"Come on, pal," the big Fed said. "You can consider it a stretch of R&R."

"I hope you're right," Bolan said.

"There'll be an embassy man at Heathrow with information for you. Are you in?"

"I'm in."

Schiphol Airport

MACK BOLAN PICKED UP the courtesy telephone.

"Belasko," he said tersely.

"Glad I caught you," Brognola answered. "Things have changed. This could turn into something heavier than just a pickup. You still in?"

"I wouldn't back off after I've come all this way. Tell me about it."

"Your man called while you were in flight. He can't make the meet. Sounds like he's in deep trouble, but he still wants to pass his information. So he's involved a friend. The only person he feels he can trust."

"A civilian?" Bolan's tone of voice reflected his concern.

"The guy had no choice. He left a message for you. Listen to it, then decide."

There was a brief silence, followed by the slight hum of a tape machine rolling.

"Belasko, this is Charlie Diel. I hate to change the play in midgame, but the bastards haven't left me any choice. They're coming out of the woodwork. More than one group. It's getting hard to ID all the players. All I can say is they're better organized than I figured. When they hit I caught a couple of bullets, and I'm losing blood. I phoned a friend by the name of Kelly McBride and asked her to meet you where we arranged. I'd already dropped the package in her In tray at the office while she was out at lunch, so hopefully no one knows she has it. Kelly's a sharp kid, and the only friend I made while I was doing my snooping. She agreed to bring you the package. I'm going to do what I can to pull the opposition away, but stay sharp, pal, because these mothers are mean. Belasko, I had to make all this up as I went along, which is why you probably figure it's ham-fisted as hell. But when you're carrying around a couple of slugs and trying to stay ahead of the bad guys, originality isn't the most important consideration. Just one more thing. The guy I tagged as the mover in this deal is a Brit named Evan Brewer. The guy is a slippery wheeler-dealer. Strictly second-rate, and this time he's in over his head. He's been playing both ends against the middle and got himself in a fix. I think he's ready to talk and cut himself a deal. He hangs out in Rotterdam. It's in my notes. He could add some weight to my report—if you can keep him alive...."

There was a long pause. All Bolan could hear was Diel's labored breathing. It was obvious that the undercover agent was in pain, fighting to stay coherent.

"Look after Kelly for me, Belasko. If you get the chance, tell her I'm sorry for getting her involved."

"That was all we got," Brognola apologized. "Diel hung up after that."

"Time I moved out," Bolan said. "Sooner I get to the rendezvous the better."

"Striker, if you need anything..."

"I'll call," Bolan said and hung up.

THE CITROËN SWERVED and came to a dead stop by the curb. Bolan glanced around the narrow street. The sidewalks were busy despite the rain. Numerous small cafés and restaurants lined the roadway, their bright neon signs splashing onto the wet pavement, the blurred colors merging.

"This is private and quiet?" Bolan asked.

McBride reached into the rear of the car and located a long tan raincoat. "It's noisy, but we can have privacy."

Bolan tucked the Uzi under the front seat as McBride struggled into the coat. He reached over and grabbed his carryall. By then his companion was out of the car. Without warning she turned in at a door and hurried down a flight of steps.

Music burst up at Bolan as he followed the woman. Hot, loud jazz drowned out most other sounds in the room. The club was dimly lighted except for the small raised dais on which the hardworking combo performed. The air was heavy with smoke—not all of it from cigarettes. Bolan was well aware of Holland's tolerance of soft drugs.

He trailed McBride across to the bar, watching as she spoke to a tall, solid man with sandy hair. It was obvious they were old friends. He glanced at Bolan, nodding, the gesture friendly.

"This way," McBride announced.

They went through a door beside the bar. McBride closed the door behind her, shutting out most of the music. She led the warrior along a passage to another door. He followed her into a cramped but neatly furnished apartment.

"It belongs to Jan Wender, the guy behind the bar."

"An old friend?"

She took off her coat and shook it.

"We've known each other for a couple of years. We met through the charity organization I work for. Jan volunteers when he can."

McBride crossed to the small kitchen area and began to fill a kettle.

"Coffee okay, Mr. Belasko?"

"Fine. And call me Mike."

"So, Mike, what have we been doing tonight?"

"Staying alive. By the way, do you have something for me from Charlie Diel?"

McBride picked up the raincoat and searched an inside pocket. She drew out a flat, wrapped package and handed it to Bolan.

"Is this worth three dead men?"

"I'll tell you when I've had a look."

Bolan sat down and opened Diel's package, which consisted of a number of handwritten sheets and several photographs. The detailed reportage had been gathered over a long period. As he scanned the information, the warrior could hear McBride moving around the kitchen. The peripheral sounds added a touch of sanity to what had already been a far-from-normal evening.

Charlie Diel had outlined his suspicions concerning illicit dealings within the charity organization Kelly McBride worked for. The Piet Sonderstrom Aid Group was committed, and had been for more than three years, to providing desperately needed food and medical supplies to the African state of Chandra.

Diel had traced the hijacked weapons as far as Holland. He had made the connection with Evan Brewer, identifying the Briton as the prime mover in the sale of the weapons. It was then that he discovered a deeper plot. The hijacked weapons, along with other arms, were being smuggled from Holland into Chandra inside the charity's supply containers.

To back his suspicions, Diel had identified a number of individuals who were part of an unholy alliance: Liam Redland—a mercenary contracted to Lenard Mdofa, an extremist violently opposed to the lawfully elected president of Chandra. Redland had been making regular visits to Amsterdam and Rotterdam for months. José Contreros—a handler for one of the Colombian drug cartels. His beat was Europe, with special interests in and around Amsterdam and the vast Europort of Rotterdam.

Diel hadn't been able to fit Contreros into the frame at first. But patient probing had uncovered information that Redland had been running a deal with Contreros to purchase drugs from the Colombians for resale. Using his own contacts, Redland had negotiated sales, moving enough narcotics to net him a huge profit, which he had used to pay for his arms purchases from Brewer. It appeared that Brewer had also acted as a go-between, conducting negotiations between the dealing parties. Diel's probing had come up with rumors that the local drug dealers were less than happy with Brewer's association with the Colombians. They had been expecting him to put them forward to Redland, especially as Brewer was in to them for substantial amounts of money forthcoming from other deals. But Brewer, with an eye for the main chance, had changed sides, courting the powerful Colombian cartel.

There was also a mention of a Star Freight Company, an outfit based in Rotterdam that had a contract with the Sonderstrom organization. Diel had placed a question mark alongside the reference, but a lack of additional information suggested he hadn't been able to follow up on his original intention.

With painstaking slowness Diel had gathered his evidence. Along with his written details, the undercover agent had added photographic proof of meetings between the main protagonists. On the rear of each photograph Diel had noted dates, places and names.

As he went through the intel, Bolan's admiration for the undercover man grew. The package in his hands represented long weeks of investigation. The agent had put himself on the line to gather his evidence, and now it appeared to have blown up in his face. Diel was out on his own, wounded and being pursued by an enemy that had already demonstrated its willingness to kill.

Bolan realized there might be little he could do to help Diel, but he could at least ensure the agent's information was put to good use.

Diel's report read like a blueprint for disaster. After reading it, Mack Bolan knew that his visit to Amsterdam had taken on a new perspective.

2

"Coffee," Kelly announced, placing a steaming mug in Bolan's hand.

He caught her steady gaze.

"Did you know that Charlie Diel was investigating the charity organization you work for?"

She shook her head. "Until he left me that package, I thought he was just another volunteer worker. That's what he'd been doing for the past few weeks. He was a friend. We worked together well. I guess he had me fooled. When he called and told me about the package and what he wanted me to do with it, well, I was surprised to say the least. But I realized he was serious, too. He wouldn't tell me what it was about in detail. All he would say was that it had something to do with the food-distribution program and certain irregularities he was looking into, but nothing Piet Sonderstrom was involved in."

"Sonderstrom is behind the program?"

"It's all down to him. He's put everything he has into the organization, Mike. He wouldn't do anything to compromise it. Right now he's on a personal tour in Canada and the U.S. trying to raise more money so we can keep the supplies rolling in."

"According to Diel, the food convoys are being used to smuggle weapons into Chandra."

"Weapons? But why?"

"Think about it, Kelly. Think about Lenard Mdofa."

"Mdofa? Of course. One of Chandra's self-styled warlords. The word is he'd do anything to get himself into power."

"Somewhere along the way Charlie Diel stumbled onto the arms dealing. Then his cover was blown. He decided Washington needed to know."

"And that's where I came in."

"Diel had already asked for a pickup because he had to get his information back to Washington. I was in London, so D.C. had me play mailman. By the time I reached the airport, Diel had already had a run-in with the opposition. Kelly, he's been shot."

"No! How badly is he hurt? Can't we help him?"

Bolan shook his head. "He knew the risks involved. His idea was to draw the opposition away while you delivered the package to me."

"Then why did those men turn up?"

"They must have been covering Diel closer than he realized. It must have occurred to them sometime that he'd dropped off at the office for a reason. Especially when they knew he was on the run. By the time they figured it out, you were already on the way. So they tailed you."

"But what about Charlie? Where is he?"

Bolan didn't answer immediately, and his silence told McBride exactly what was going through his mind.

"You think he's dead?"

"If they find him, he isn't going to walk out with his hands up. He'll do everything he can to avoid telling them what he's found out."

"God, Mike, it's horrible."

"It's called covering all the bases."

"I don't care what it's called. How do we stop these people? And why are they so desperate to hush things up?"

"Good question. The way things are moving, maybe Chandra is closer to flash point than we realize."

"Well, right now it's in the grip of a drought that's been ongoing for almost three years. There's intertribal rivalry and political unease. Victor Joffi is the only man capable of holding everything together."

"If he's allowed to."

"Mdofa will do anything to topple the government. He believes it's his destiny to rule the country. The fact that he's hated by the majority of the population doesn't worry him. In Chandra power is everything. The man who holds the highest office has the right to rule. It goes back to the times of the old tribal chiefs. Mdofa has enough influential backers to maintain his position if he does reach the presidential palace. Plus his private army of bullyboys."

"What about the people?"

"They can barely survive because of the drought. Chandra doesn't produce much—a few crops, cattle. The country is still primitive. The population is too scattered to pose any threat to someone like Mdofa. He has his eye on lining his pockets. There are healthy copper deposits in the north just waiting for development. If Mdofa gains control he'll run the country like a feudal state. His chosen followers will live in luxury while the rest work for starvation wages."

"Sounds like a familiar story."

"Not if I have anything to do with it," McBride snapped defiantly.

"It isn't as easy as that."

"Coming from someone who shot three people tonight... Just who do you work for, Mike Belasko? And don't tell me the NYPD."

"The U.S. government."

"So does Smokey the Bear, only he doesn't carry a gun and use it the way you do."

"The lady has a point," said someone behind Bolan.

The warrior turned, his hand moving in the direction of the holstered Beretta.

"I wouldn't."

The speaker was a suntanned man with a mop of thick hair spilling over his coat collar. He held an Uzi in his right hand, and the muzzle of the weapon was pressed into Jan Wender's neck. The pair was standing in the open doorway of the apartment.

"Take the hand away from the gun, mate," the armed man ordered. His accent was hard and flat, telling Bolan he came from the north of England. His movements and attitude told the Executioner he'd had military experience.

The gunner pushed Jan ahead of him into the room. Bolan saw a second hardman crowd in behind him, close the door and stand with his back against it.

"This is cozy," the dark-haired man said. He pushed Wender away from him, then moved the Uzi so it covered Bolan and McBride. "You've been busy tonight, love," he said to the woman. "Led us a right bloody dance."

"Go to hell. Just what do you think you're playing at?"

The dark-haired man turned his gaze on her, studying her supple figure. His thoughts showed in his narrow eyes, and the woman flushed.

"We're not playing games, love. This is for real. Maybe you'd like to be dead. Your chum, here, saw off three of my pals tonight. He knows what it's all about. You watch too much American TV. Get hit tonight and it will hurt, and I mean hurt. Bugger me about and I'll do things to that pretty face you'll never forget."

McBride shrank from his threat.

A few feet away Wender muttered something Bolan couldn't hear, then took a step toward the dark-haired gunman.

"Bloody well don't!" the man yelled, pulling the muzzle of his Uzi away from Bolan.

The warrior plunged his hand under his jacket, withdrew the 93-R and aimed it at the man standing by the door. The hardman had been listening to the words flying between McBride and his partner, and he had allowed his concentration to slip. Bolan didn't allow him the chance to tighten it up. He stroked the trigger and a 3-round burst drilled into the guy's skull, dappling the wall at his side with bloody debris.

The dark-haired gunman swore vehemently and pulled back from Wender, intending to deal with Bolan.

Kelly McBride stepped into the fray, swinging her right arm up and around, emptying her mug of hot coffee into the gunman's face.

He let out a strangled screech, bringing up his left arm to scrub at the hot liquid stinging his eyes and face.

The Executioner pushed himself forward, ducking under the barrel of the Uzi, and slammed his right shoulder into the gunman's side. The impact of the blow cracked a rib and drove the guy across the room. He stumbled over the leg of a chair and went down on his knees. He attempted to raise the Uzi, but Bolan's swinging right foot caught him a glancing blow under the chin. The force snapped his jaws together, chipping teeth. As the hardman crashed to the floor, the Executioner wrenched the Uzi out of his hand.

He caught hold of his adversary's shirt and hauled him to his feet, shoving him back across the room until the gunman came to a stop against the wall, with the muzzle of Bolan's 93-R screwing into the flesh of his cheek.

"Still feel cozy, *mate?*" the warrior growled.

"Been worse off," the man grunted through pursed lips, ignoring the gun and slamming a knee into the Executioner's groin.

Bolan doubled over. As a wave of nausea swept over him, he sensed his opponent gathering himself for an attack.

The warrior dropped to one knee a moment before the hardman slammed both fists toward the back of his neck. Absorbing the impact, Bolan gathered himself and straightened, catching his adversary bent over him. The gunman was lifted off his feet, then spun over Bolan's body as the Executioner grasped one of his arms and pulled. The guy was dropped to the floor on his back. He rolled, backpedaling as he tried to reach his feet, simultaneously clawing under his jacket for a backup weapon.

Bolan saw the squat handgun glint in the lamplight. He took a dive in the direction of the floor, hearing the hard crack of the gun. The bullet burned the air above his head, drilling into the far wall. Coming up on one knee the warrior leveled the Beretta. His finger touched the trigger, and the suppressed autopistol released a triburst. The 9 mm tumblers ravaged the gunman's chest, dropping him to the floor in an untidy heap.

As Bolan climbed to his feet, he winced at the pain in his groin. That one had hurt.

"Any more of them out there, Jan?" he asked.

Wender shrugged. "All I can tell you is he was at the bar. He had that Uzi under his coat, showed it to me and said to stay calm and to bring him to you. What else could I do with all those people out there?"

"You did right," Bolan said. He picked up one of the discarded Uzis.

"Jan, I'm sorry this had to happen," McBride said. "I wouldn't have come if—"

"That doesn't matter. Just tell me what I can do to help."

"They'll have Kelly's car spotted," Bolan said, "and I'm betting there'll be someone outside watching it now. Can we get out any other way?"

Wender nodded. "Fire door at the rear." He reached into his pocket and pulled out a key. "Take my car. Kelly knows it."

"What about these?" McBride indicated the two dead gunmen.

Bolan looked around and located a telephone and dialed a number.

"I need Stewart," he said when the connection was made. "Tell him it's Belasko."

While he waited Bolan turned to Kelly.

"Write down the address of this place."

She did as he asked, handing him the slip of paper.

"Stewart? Listen and don't ask questions. The pickup has gone hard. Diel's out on his own somewhere. I need a cleanup at this address—" he read out the information McBride had provided "—and some protection for a friendly named Jan Wender. Pass this to home base. I need to stay on the move right now. I'll call in when I can."

Bolan dropped the receiver. He tucked Diel's report into its envelope, stuffed it inside his leather jacket, pulled up the zip, then picked up his carryall.

"Some people from the U.S. Consulate will drop by. The guy in charge will be named Stewart. They'll clear up this mess."

McBride grabbed Wender's arm and kissed him on the cheek. "Thanks."

Bolan shook the man's hand, then guided McBride out the door and down the passage, in the direction

Wender indicated. The fire door opened onto the club's delivery area, and a number of parked cars. The woman hurried to a black BMW, unlocked the driver's door and slipped behind the wheel. The Executioner moved around the car to the passenger door and slid in beside her.

McBride dropped the gears into reverse and spun the heavy car, then guided the vehicle along the rear of the building toward the street.

"Where are we going?"

"Where do your food shipments leave Holland?"

"Rotterdam."

"Then we need to go there," Bolan said. "If I can confirm Diel's story, we'll have something to move on. If the weapons go out in the supply containers, then Rotterdam is the place to look. And there's a man I need to find by the name of Evan Brewer. He's an Englishman who arranged the arms deal and one or two other things according to Diel's information."

"There is a consignment ready to be shipped out the day after tomorrow. You're saying there might be weapons hidden in the containers?"

"It's possible," Bolan replied.

As McBride braked before turning onto the street, Bolan caught sight of rapid movement in the rearview mirror. A running figure emerged from the fire door and cut along the alley in their direction.

"Let's go!" Bolan snapped. "Get us out of here."

McBride didn't question his order. She stepped on the gas pedal and sent the powerful BMW surging along the street.

The warrior twisted, peering through the spray that was arcing up from the BMW's tires. Back along the street he made out Kelly's red Citroën. Just beyond it was a car with its lights on. The figure from the alley emerged, waving frantically, and seconds later the idling car began to move. It paused long enough to pick up the waiting figure, then accelerated.

"Are you a good driver, Kelly?" Bolan asked, checking the Uzi he'd picked up in Wender's apartment.

"Let's say we're both going to find out."

3

"These guys are well organized," Bolan said. "This is the second time they've tagged us."

He glanced hard at McBride until the woman turned her head to glare at him.

"What?" she asked sharply. "Are you suggesting I'm leading them to us?"

"Just keep your eyes on the road," the Executioner cautioned. "All I have to go on, Kelly, is what's happened since I landed in Holland. A simple pickup turns into a shooting match. We head for a safehouse and the opposition turns up there, as well. They either have a damn good backup service running in Amsterdam, or they're using a crystal ball. Personally I don't rate crystal balls, so that leaves us with their security arm."

"Okay," McBride agreed, swinging the BMW around a sharp bend. "Maybe I did lead them to the first meeting. But how did they latch on to Jan's place so fast? You think they bugged my car or something?"

"It's possible."

"Great," the woman muttered. "Not doing too well my first day on the job, am I?"

"It happens to the best of us. You seem to be handling the rest pretty well."

"Working in Chandra, you get used to seeing death on a daily basis. Not all of it from starvation. It's a beautiful country, but it's going through hell at the moment. Has for the past few years. Having our food convoys stopped at gunpoint has become a regular thing. And seeing people getting shot isn't new to me. I don't like it, but it's part of the job."

She took the BMW down a narrow side street, cutting between parked cars with inches to spare, and braked only briefly as she made a sharp right.

"They're still with us," Bolan told her as the pursuit car skidded into view and locked on their tail again.

The rear window of the BMW shattered as a bullet punched through it, plowing into the padded rear of Bolan's seat.

McBride hauled on the wheel and took the car up a narrow alley, raising sparks as the near-side fender of the BMW scraped against the wall. They emerged in the loading area of business premises that were closed for the night, with stacked crates and barrels filling most of the space.

"Damn!" McBride yelled when she realized they were boxed in.

"Hit the brakes!" Bolan ordered.

He slipped the safety off the Uzi and was freeing the door lock even as McBride touched the brakes, sending the BMW into a slow broadside. The warrior kicked the door open and exited the vehicle, hitting the wet ground on his left shoulder and rolling away from the car. He checked himself, coming up in a combat crouch, and saw the chase car round the end of the building, headlights cutting white arcs through the rainy shadows.

Tires slithered on the concrete as the wheels locked, the driver fighting the car's slide. The hardman leaning out of the passenger window attempted to take out Bolan. He triggered a panic burst when he spotted the crouching Executioner, the stream of suppressed slugs passing over the warrior's head to shatter a window behind him.

Bolan stitched the halted vehicle with a sustained burst from the Uzi, bringing the muzzle up to window level, driving the armed passenger back inside. As the lethal spray of 9 mm slugs found their targets, the driver and passenger twisted and jerked in silent protest, flesh and bones ravaged by the deadly volley.

The Executioner closed on the chase car. When he pulled open the closed door, the interior light came on, illuminating the scene. Both men were dead, their riddled bodies broken and bleeding.

Coming up behind the Executioner, carrying his carryall, Kelly McBride barely repressed a horrified gasp. Just as swiftly she recovered.

"Mike, I know the one behind the wheel. I've seen him at the Rotterdam warehouse. He works for the freight company that hauls the supply containers for the aid group."

As she spoke, Bolan stowed the Uzi in his carryall. He closed the bag, grabbed McBride's arm and hurried her across the yard and down a narrow, dark alley. The lane twisted and wound between high-walled buildings that lay in shadow. When they finally emerged they stood on a cobbled street that held a succession of small shops, dark and closed now, with only the soft glow of street lamps to break the misty gloom. Bolan maintained his hold on his companion's arm and they walked at a steady, unhurried pace along the street.

"Any idea where we are?" the warrior asked.

McBride glanced around until she located a street sign. "Okay, I recognize the area."

"How close are we to the rail station?"

"About ten minutes I'd guess."

"Let's go," Bolan said.

They continued along the street, to all outward appearances just another couple caught in the rain as they walked, heads down, busy with their own thoughts.

Mack Bolan's thoughts were far removed from any worries about the rain. He was trying to make sense out of everything that had happened since his arrival in Holland.

The information Charlie Diel had uncovered seemed to have stirred up a hornet's nest. If, as the undercover agent's report indicated, an arms-smuggling ring was using the Piet Sonderstrom charity as cover, it looked more than probable that Diel's investigation had occurred during a delicate stage in the operation, which would explain the desperate attempts to silence both Bolan and Kelly McBride.

Someone had panicked, and that panic had been manifested in the relentless attacks. Bolan's success in staving off his adversaries would only push the opposition to greater efforts.

Like it or not, Bolan was committed now. He had the knowledge Diel's undercover operation had brought to light, and if his brief talk with Kelly—concerning Lenard Mdofa—was correct, then the warrior had no choice other than to follow through and bring a degree of justice into the game—Executioner-style.

4

Brad Dekker was sweating and squirming.

He'd been sweating before he reached Liam Redland's office. The squirming had been brought on by Redland's impassive, cold expression. The last time he had been made aware of that look, Dekker had been on a dusty plain in Chandra seconds before Redland had personally executed two of Mdofa's soldiers. The execution had been ordered by the African as an example to others in his force that betrayal was something never to be tolerated. Redland had carried out the executions, using his own handgun, at close range, and hadn't turned a hair as he had blown out the brains of the unfortunate troopers.

It had been the look in Redland's eyes that had disturbed Dekker more than the actual killing, and he was seeing that same look now.

Redland jerked a finger at a seat next to his desk, and Dekker sat, casting his gaze over the others already ranged around the office. They were all silent and looked as uncomfortable as Dekker himself felt.

"Now that we're all here," Redland said, "maybe we can sort out this bloody mess."

He glanced at Dekker, fixing him with his unblinking stare.

Dekker thought briefly about shooting the man if all the blame was laid at his door. The plan of action comforted him, but only for a few pleasant moments. Then he dragged himself back to the present and the real world.

"What's the word from the streets?" Redland asked.

"Tyrone and Gjent took off after this Belasko—he's the one Diel was going to pass his information to—and the woman when they left the jazz club. They left Kramer to check the place out. Belasko left two of our boys dead in the club."

"That's it?"

"More or less."

Redland leaned back in his seat. "Did Belasko or McBride contact anyone in the club?"

"A guy behind the bar who runs the place. He's a part-time helper at the Amsterdam offices of the Sonderstrom organization."

"Maybe we should talk to him."

"Good thought, Liam, but he took off when Kramer ran across him. He took the McBride woman's car."

"Better and bloody better," Redland growled. "Now we've got another loose cannon running around Amsterdam. For God's sake get somebody on this bar guy."

Dekker nodded. "Eddie, go arrange it."

He turned to one of the other men. "Contact Contreros. Ask him to get his people to cover the streets. He's got enough of them."

After Eddie had left the office, Redland sat forward, his hands flat on the desktop.

"This Belasko is running rings around you people." His gaze passed over every face in the room, and to a man they all avoided direct eye contact with him. "And there I was believing I'd hired the best. Must have been an off day when I picked you guys. We'll have to do better when we get back to Chandra. Mdofa isn't going to be as tolerant as I am."

"Liam, Belasko is no beginner," Dekker protested, regretting the words as soon as they left his mouth.

"I'm sure we're all agreed on that," Redland replied. "The question is who *are* the beginners?"

Redland slammed one hand on the desktop.

"Now listen good, because I don't intend repeating myself. I want you on this now. We can't afford to have this Belasko character running around loose if he's carrying information Charlie Diel compiled. Now that Diel's dead there's one less to worry about. But this thing with Brewer is getting out of hand. The son of a bitch got us guns hijacked from the U.S. government, and Diel got wind of it. The last thing we need is an investigation by the Americans. I want Brewer dead. That bastard is responsible for everything blowing up in our faces. I wouldn't have touched his deal if I'd known where the weapons had come from. Our intel was too slow picking that up. Diel wasn't. I don't want Brewer spilling his guts to Belasko. We can't afford to run up against the Americans right now. There's too much going on in Chandra. We're close to the main event, so I don't want anything getting through to give Joffi a sniff of what's in the wind. We're going to have to move the shipment forward, get it out as fast as we can.''

"These things happen, Liam," Dekker said, trying to placate the man.

"Not to me they bloody well don't!" Redland yelled. "Not this close to a takeover in Chandra."

"You sure you want Belasko alive? It would be easier to finish him off."

"We need him alive for now. At least until we can figure out how far Diel's information has gone. Diel made sure we had to kill him once he was cornered so he wouldn't talk. And, yes, we need the woman. If she isn't too much for you to handle. We might be able to use her to persuade Belasko to talk if he decides to be stubborn. Another thing—try and keep it low-key. Too many firefights on the streets isn't the best way to avoid being noticed."

"Belasko isn't shy at pulling the trigger," said one of the men facing Redland across the room. "Look how many we've lost already."

Redland considered for a moment. "He's got the advantage. Drawing attention makes it harder for us."

"Maybe it's time to call in some favors," Dekker suggested.

"Meaning?"

"We've got people bought and paid for. It's time to collect."

Redland smiled. "You're starting to think, Dek. Much more of that and I'll have to watch *my* back."

MINUTES LATER Dekker, in another room, picked up the telephone and dialed a number.

While he waited for the call to be answered, his mind was going over the recent events in Redland's office. Okay, so Redland was the leader of the outfit. That didn't mean he could treat people like dirt. Making his men look small wasn't the way to keep them loyal—not when it came to putting their lives on the line. Liam Redland was a hard bastard, no question, but he had a lot to learn when it came to handling his own men.

The main reason everyone put up with his abuse was the fact that they were being paid good money. Lenard Mdofa, the man footing the payroll bill, was far from mean where money was concerned. It meant that a lot of the people working to get him into the top position in Chandra were only in it for the amount they could make, which made them slightly unreliable.

Mdofa believed that money could get him anything he wanted. He was correct up to a point. In the long term, however, if the money began to dry up, Mdofa was going to find himself running Chandra on his own. Dekker wasn't overly concerned about that. He had signed on only for the takeover. Once Mdofa was installed, Dekker, along with most of the other mercenaries, would be shipping out, searching for another contract.

And that was where Redland *was* going to have to watch his back. If he kept on mishandling his men, he might find he had a permanent spot in Chandra—six feet underground.

The phone clicked as the distant receiver was lifted.

"Hello."

"Can you talk?" Dekker asked.

"Yes."

"It's payday. I'm collecting."

There was a slight pause. "Go ahead."

"First I need a trace."

"Give me the details."

5

The square fronting the station was nearly deserted due to the rain. During dry days and warm evenings, the wide square offered impromptu performances from street entertainers, attracting crowds of sightseers. This evening the slabbed square glistened with rain. Anyone passing by hurried across the open area, or headed for the shelter of the station's interior.

Mack Bolan glanced at his watch as he and Kelly McBride crossed the square. It was just coming up to 8:45 p.m. Bolan's eyes scanned the square and the area adjoining. Traffic on the streets moved by purposefully. No one wanted to linger any longer than necessary on such a dreary evening. Even so, Bolan scrutinized each vehicle until he was sure there was no threat.

The ornate sculpted stone panels on either side of the main entrance dripped with rain. Bolan noticed a couple of raincoated figures hovering near the head of the steps that led down to the subway station. He slipped his hand inside his unzipped leather jacket, curling his fingers around the Beretta's grips. One of the figures moved, leaning toward the other. A match flared, and a cigarette was lighted. The man drew away from the match, blowing out smoke. He nodded to his companion, and the two vanished from sight down the steps. Bolan let out a sharp breath, relieving the tension.

They entered the station, and Bolan's awareness heightened again. This was the sort of place liable to be under scrutiny by the opposition. If the Executioner had been doing the stalking, he would have staked out the station and the bus depot, trying to cover the most likely places someone on the move might use. By now the abandoned BMW would have been located, and someone would have latched on to the fact that Bolan and McBride were on foot.

It wasn't high intelligence, just simple logic and the elimination of other avenues of escape.

Bolan pulled Dutch gulden notes from his pocket, courtesy of the U.S. Embassy in London, and passed them to McBride.

"Two tickets to Rotterdam on the next train," he said.

She nodded and walked to the ticket booth. Bolan watched her and scanned the concourse, looking for anyone paying too much attention to her.

He almost missed the skinny long-haired man dressed in dirty jeans and an old army combat jacket. The guy pretended to study the newspaper he was holding, but his eyes were on McBride. He watched her buy the tickets, then turn away from the booth. Bolan approached the woman, not letting on he had spotted the lookout. When she reached the warrior, he took her arm and guided her across the concourse to a cigarette machine.

"I don't smoke," she protested.

"Buy some anyway," he instructed. "We're being watched. The skinny guy in a combat jacket and jeans."

"He doesn't sound like one of my friends."

"How long do we have before our train leaves?"

"An hour."

"Long enough," Bolan said.

McBride fiddled with the cigarettes she had just purchased. She followed Bolan as he recrossed the concourse, making for the exit. The warrior shoved the carryall into McBride's arms.

The moment they stepped onto the square Bolan made a quick turn to the left, pulling the woman behind him and pushing her against the wall. She had the quick wits to remain silent.

Moments later the man in the combat jacket stepped into view, muttering into a compact mobile phone.

Bolan slapped it out of his hand. The phone clattered to the ground, skidding across the wet slabs. The guy began to protest, but the Executioner caught hold of his jacket, swung him around and slammed him back against the wall. The guy coughed as his breath burst from his lungs. When he recovered he looked up and found himself staring into the muzzle of Bolan's 9 mm Beretta.

"You're very close, pal," Bolan advised, "so don't take the final step."

"I don't know—"

Bolan placed the muzzle of the 93-R against the guy's nose.

"Don't insult me. We both know what you're up to. What you *were* up to. You quit for the rest of the night, or you quit for the rest of your life. The choice is yours. Either way doesn't bother me.''

The man stared into Bolan's cold eyes and had a vision of death. It was as near as he wanted to get at that point of his life, so he chose the easy path for the time being.

"Okay, I'm out of it."

Bolan took the guy's reply without comment, not believing him for a second.

"One question. Who are you running for, Redland or a hometown team?''

The guy stared down at the Beretta, then up at Bolan's face.

"You can kill me," he said weakly. "I'm dead if I tell you anyway.''

The warrior saw the fear in the guy's eyes. His gaunt face was stark white.

On an impulse Bolan grabbed his prisoner's sleeve and pushed it up his bony arm until it reached the elbow. Even in the dim light he was able to see the needle marks, the open sores and the scabbed ones.

The guy was an addict, probably a dealer, too, who got paid in dope to feed his own habit. He'd probably been promised a large bonus in the form of white powder to act as a lookout for Bolan and McBride.

Another link in the chain. Charlie Diel's intel had mentioned drugs.

He ground the Beretta hard against the guy's nose, bringing tears to the watery blue eyes.

"You tell your people to stay away from me, or I'll tear this town apart to get to them.''

The skinny man nodded, seeming to acquiesce to Bolan's demand. The Executioner caught a glimmer of defiance in his eyes and braced himself for any sudden move the guy might make.

"Get out of here," Bolan said icily, stepping back from the man.

The lookout moved away from the wall, pausing, then bending to retrieve the mobile phone.

"Leave it!"

The man curled his fingers, then started to straighten.

His move came swiftly. His hand passed over the top of his left boot, and when he stood upright, a slim-bladed knife jutted from his hand. He made a low, slashing cut with the knife, aiming for Bolan's stomach.

The warrior had been prepared for the move. He eased back, lifted his right foot and slammed the toe of his shoe against the guy's wrist. Bone snapped and the knife slipped from nerveless fingers. Bolan moved in close, lifting his foot a second time and planting it in the small of his adversary's back. He shoved hard, sending the guy staggering forward. With a brief yell he vanished down the steps.

Bolan jammed the Beretta back into its holster. He snatched up the mobile phone and turned to Kelly.

"Let's go," he said.

"Wrong way," she pointed out as the warrior headed away from the station.

"He might have already told someone we were going to use the train. If we turn up in Rotterdam, there'll be a welcoming committee waiting for us at the station.''

"So where *are* we going?"

"To Rotterdam, but by a different route."

They walked across the square, following the line of the station, then cut across the street.

"How do we know someone isn't following us right now?"

"We don't," Bolan answered.

It was the honest truth. If Redland was using the street runners belonging to a drug syndicate to spot for him, there could be half a dozen pairs of eyes on them at any one time.

"Mike, this is hopeless. Why don't we get in touch with the Amsterdam police, tell them what's been going on and . . ."

Bolan shook his head. "Right now the only person I trust in this town is you."

"Are you saying the police can't be trusted?"

"It wouldn't be the first time police officials have been bought by the drug syndicates. We don't have time to play around looking for the good guys."

They had emerged on a street running alongside one of the canals. Bolan slowed his pace, eyeing the lines of cars parked there. He checked them out until he spotted an elderly Renault. Easing alongside the car, he made a quick check of its doors. One of the rear ones was unlocked. He reached in and unlocked the front door, then slipped in behind the wheel.

As McBride got into the passenger seat, Bolan reached under the dash and located the wiring. It took him no more than thirty seconds to hot-wire the ignition. There was a brief crackle as he connected the exposed wires, then the engine coughed sluggishly and caught. Bolan touched the gas pedal and the revs built to a healthy grumble. He eased off the parking brake, dropped into first gear and rolled the Renault along the wet cobbles.

"Rotterdam?"

McBride provided precise instructions, guiding him through the city and onto the cross-country highway linking Amsterdam with Rotterdam.

The warrior stared at the mobile phone resting on the dashboard, where he had placed it. The guy had been making a call when he had walked into Bolan's hands. A report to his employer to let him know that he'd tagged the marks?

Bolan picked it up and scanned the keypad. In the bottom right-hand corner was a redial button; when pressed it automatically dialed the last number keyed in. Bolan thumbed it, heard the numbers click off, then picked up the ring tone.

The phone was answered by a man speaking in heavily accented English, but not Dutch-accented. The man speaking had the richer, flowing accent that could only have originated in South America, as in Colombia.

And Colombia, in this instance, was most likely to be connected to José Contreros, the Colombian drug dealer Diel had reported being involved with Redland and Evan Brewer.

MOMENTS AFTER BOLAN had driven the Renault into the rain-streaked darkness, a pale young woman clad in soaked clothing that clung to her emaciated figure raised a mobile phone to her lips. She had witnessed Bolan's interception of the tail outside the railway station, and had followed the American and his red-haired companion when they had abandoned the station in favor of a stolen vehicle. The woman, a drug addict totally dependent on the deadly narcotics supplied to her by the Colombian dealers, relayed her information to her contact. The information detailed the Renault, its license number and the new occupants. The young woman's information would net her a few days' supply of cocaine. Though she didn't know it, she was already on the relentless downward spiral that would eventually claim her life. Within the year she would be dead, another victim of the white powder that brought nothing but misery and suffering to its users and untold wealth to the calculating men who sold it. Her death would be noted and cataloged, just another statistic in the continuing disease known as the drug trade. No one would be brought to justice over her death.

The number the young woman called was the same one Mack Bolan had unknowingly used when he had keyed the redial button on the mobile phone taken from the tail outside the station. The man who answered was the same one Bolan had heard....

6

Bolan didn't speak until they were clear of the city. He drove steadily, keeping well inside the speed limit. The last thing he needed was to get pulled over by some zealous Dutch cop and given a ticket. Especially as he was driving a stolen car and carrying a loaded gun.

Sensing his mood, McBride held her own silence for as long as she could. The involvement of the drug traffickers added a new complication to an already-involved series of events.

She was aware of her companion's mood. He was deep in thought, and McBride suspected he was deliberating on his next move. Whatever it might be, she felt certain he would handle it well. He had already demonstrated he was no newcomer when it came to sudden life or death situations.

"We're going to need gas soon," Bolan said suddenly.

The woman peered through the rain-streaked windshield at a sign coming up.

"You can take the next side road. There's a gas station about two miles along."

Bolan eased the Renault off the main highway and soon after picked out the lights of the gas station. He rolled the car onto the concrete island and braked beside a pump. He broke the wired ignition and let the engine stop. Climbing out, he moved to the self-service pump and began to fill the tank. He almost missed the parked car sitting just out of the pool of light beyond the station. Although it had its lights off, Bolan recognized the telltale outline of a roof-flasher unit. A police patrol cruiser.

Continuing to fill the tank, Bolan tapped gently on the car's roof to attract his companion's attention.

"What is it?"

"Just climb out and join me."

Bolan pulled several bills from his pocket and handed them to her.

"Go pay the guy," he said.

"What's up?"

"There's a police car off to the right, beyond the island. Don't look. Just take my word. They might be on a routine patrol. Taking a break."

"But they could be on the lookout for us."

"I could be wrong. For all we know this car might not have been missed yet. Then again, maybe the number has already been circulated."

"So what do we do?"

"We pay for the gas and roll on out of here. As soon as possible we lose this car and find something else."

McBride strolled to the booth and paid the attendant. He took the money with barely a glance at her. By the time she returned to the car, Bolan had the engine ticking over. He eased away from the station, keeping one eye on the dark outline of the stationary police car. Approaching the highway, Bolan slowed to see if the cruiser was tailing them. The road behind them remained deserted.

"I don't like this setup," Bolan commented as he pushed the Renault up to the speed limit, his gaze searching the way ahead as well as the road behind them. "Something about it doesn't read right."

"Like you expect something to happen even though the signs tell you it's okay?"

"Exactly."

"I get that feeling when we're running the food convoys through the bush in Chandra. And every time I do, something does happen."

Bolan continually monitored the clock on the dashboard, watching the minutes slip by as they sped in the direction of Rotterdam. Something had to happen soon. Ten minutes stretched to twenty, then to a half hour.

Still nothing.

The highway stretched before them, the surface glistening in the glare from the headlights. There was little traffic at this hour. When Bolan picked up the twin beams of a car behind them, his gut feeling told him to expect the worst when the car made no attempt to close up or pass them. He lowered his speed, and the tail car dropped back itself. Minutes later a second car appeared ahead of them, and Bolan realized they were boxed in.

Now the tail car began to close up, pushing dangerously close to the Renault's rear. It was a classic move. Each vehicle, ahead and behind, was able to maneuver so that Bolan was kept from dropping back or accelerating.

McBride, aware of the situation, sat tight. She said nothing, not wanting to distract Bolan in any way.

The warrior pulled his seat belt tight, then dropped his hand to the gearshift. McBride snugged her own belt and felt the Renault surge forward as Bolan dropped into a lower gear and trod on the gas pedal. The driver ahead realized a split second too late what Bolan was doing. He tried to pull away, but the Renault rear-ended him.

Dragging tires screeched as the lead car was pushed off course. Bolan kept up the pressure, forcing the other car to broadside. He let go of the pedal long enough to drop back a fraction, then hit the power again. The Renault's battered nose slammed into the other car, catching it just behind the rear door. Bolan poured on the gas, shoving the lead car into a three-quarter circle, then hauled on the wheel and took the Renault clear. He powered away, aware that the tail car was still around and taking up the chase.

As he sped along the highway, Bolan glanced in his rearview mirror. The lead car was motionless, skewed across the road and not moving. But the tail car was closing fast.

"I don't think we'll outrun him, Mike," McBride said. "He's moving really fast."

The tail car closed with chilling speed, swerving to Bolan's side. An armed figure appeared in the rear door's window, thrusting a stubby shape into view. Muzzle-flashes lighted up the darkness as the autoweapon opened fire, slugs sparking off the road's surface just short of the Renault.

"He's trying for the tires," Bolan commented.

Freeing one hand from the wheel, the Executioner unzipped the carryall and pulled out the Uzi. He ejected the magazine, snapped in one of the reserves he was carrying and pulled back the cocking bolt. Bolan rolled down the window and laid the Uzi across the sill, slamming on the brakes when the chase car filled his field of vision. The moment the other car drew level Bolan triggered the Uzi, weaving a full-auto pattern at the windshield and the closest window. Slugs shattered glass and steel, filling the interior with deadly shards. The car lurched aside, running full tilt into the median. It scraped along, trailing a brilliant rainbow of sparks, until the front wheels spun it clear. It hurtled across the highway, then flipped and rolled. Bouncing and shedding debris, it ran out of highway and vanished over the guardrail. Moments later a glowing ball of flame blazed into the night sky.

Bolan closed his window. He dropped the Uzi to the floor of the Renault and set the car back along the empty highway.

"I'll say one thing, Mike Belasko. A night out with you is anything but dull."

"It's the company I keep."

Even as he spoke Bolan's mind was racing ahead, anticipating the opposition's next move. Someone was feeding them information on his whereabouts. The speed in which they had been picked up this time suggested that radio contact was being used. If that was so, then they could expect more company before they reached Rotterdam. In that case it might be a wise move to lose the Renault and take alternative transport into the city.

"If we don't pick up another tail by the next exit," he said, "I want to get off the highway. We can hide this car and get into Rotterdam some other way."

McBride nodded as she studied the roadside directions.

"Okay, in about twenty minutes we'll pick up the signs for Leiden. We'll be able to lose ourselves once we dump this thing."

When the signs appeared, Bolan took the exit ramp and followed the road to Leiden. He eventually spotted a large hotel, its parking lot well lighted. He pulled in and slotted the Renault in the far corner.

"We registering for the night?" McBride asked.

"No. Find a phone and call a cab to take us to Rotterdam."

The woman went into the hotel lobby, where she located a bank of pay phones. While she called for the taxi, Bolan hovered near the entrance, out of the constant drizzle, and watched for signs of trouble. He expected it.

"The cab will be here in five minutes," McBride told him when she returned from the telephone. "They were reluctant to go as far as Rotterdam this late at night, but I promised a big tip. Can you afford it?"

Bolan nodded. Money was the least of his worries.

He was reviewing his list of priorities. The Executioner wanted to make contact with Evan Brewer to find out what the man had to offer. And Rotterdam would present him with the opportunity to check out the supply containers intended for Chandra.

He didn't know what he was going to find, other than a hostile reception. The warrior would have expected nothing less. The people he was going up against were predators. They had attached themselves to the Piet Sonderstrom organization and were using its humanitarian facilities to import death and destruction into a country already on the brink of starvation. The suffering of the Chandran population meant nothing. They were preparing to unleash a bloody coup against the existing administration in order to establish a dictatorship that would extend the nation's suffering. The man working for Lenard Mdofa had already showed they had few scruples when it came to financing their cause. Drugs had been bought, traded and sold in order to raise cash. The drugs, probably already distributed, would create more misery and suffering when they reached their destination. The whole package added up to large-scale evil.

The only balance that had been introduced—albeit by default—was the presence of Mack Bolan. He had dealt himself into the game, not just because he had been drawn into a trap in Amsterdam, but due in part to Charlie Diel's obvious death at the hands of the enemy and his subsequent insight into what they were prepared to do to gain their objectives.

Bolan couldn't have walked away now. He was, as ever, totally committed to yet another battle in his War Everlasting.

The next skirmish would commence somewhere in Rotterdam.

7

A chill wind drifted in off the Meuse River, bordering the city of Rotterdam. The wind added to the discomfort of the rain that continued to fall from the overcast late-night sky.

Mack Bolan, shoulders hunched under his leather jacket, followed Kelly McBride through the gate of the dockside facility housing the Piet Sonderstrom storage and distribution center. The night watchman on the gate had recognized McBride immediately, and they had no problem getting onto the dock. There was little activity taking place, though security lights blazed at regular intervals. A number of container units stood on the dockside, waiting to be loaded on the freighter that was due to berth within the next couple of days.

They entered the administration building and climbed the stairs that led to the warehouse manager's office. Here the loading of the containers was monitored, each load checked and placed on a manifest. The containers were inspected and signed for by the Dutch customs department, then sealed before loading.

In the cramped office, McBride pulled out of a pigeonhole the stack of manifests listing the cargo that was to be loaded the following day.

"These have all been checked and sealed, Mike."

She took him to the window overlooking the dock and indicated the line of containers sitting there. Each container bore lettering that displayed the freight company logo, container size and weight, and also a number to match the manifests.

"Each container has its own number that corresponds to an individual manifest detailing the contents. Ten containers, ten manifests."

"I only count nine," Bolan observed.

McBride rechecked the forms.

"Container 168 is at the freight company workshop," she stated, reading the detail at the bottom of the manifest. "It's a refrigerated container. Says here there was a problem with the coolant system. It had to go back to be fixed."

"What do they need to keep cool?"

"We always take in medicine with the food convoys—antibiotics, serums, the kind of medication that has to be kept cool to stop deterioration. The fridge container is kept working during the voyage, and as soon as it arrives in Chandra the tractor unit takes over."

Bolan made no comment.

"Mike? What are you thinking?"

"You recognized one of the men in that chase car back in Amsterdam. Remember? You told me he worked for the freight company handling the containers."

"They're involved?"

"It looks possible now. How deeply, I don't know. But at least it gives us a link, which needs to be followed up."

"Okay," the woman said, moving toward the door.

"Not this time, Kelly. I want you somewhere safe. I need to be on my own when I make my visit to the freight company."

McBride didn't raise any objections. She was aware that every time danger threatened, the man she knew as Mike Belasko was sacrificing a degree of his own safety in order to protect her. For what he intended to do next—and there was a distinct possibility that a violent reaction might occur—he needed to be in complete control.

"So where do you want me to go, Mike?"

JUST OVER AN HOUR LATER Mack Bolan was crouched in the shadows close to the security chain-link fence that surrounded the compound that housed the Star Freight Company.

From the dockside, he and McBride had taken a taxi to a quiet, side-street hotel off the A4 highway. The hotel was the kind whose personnel didn't ask too many questions, and the money Bolan produced got them a room. As soon as McBride was settled, he had left.

Picking up another taxi, and armed with the location of the freight company, the warrior had settled in the back seat, taking the opportunity to relax before pushing himself into the fray once more.

He also took the opportunity to delve further into Charlie Diel's background information on the weapons-drug connection.

At first the whole business appeared too complex to be feasible. Closer examination of the small print allowed the tangled strands to be separated, revealing a fairly straightforward progression.

Mdofa's representative in Holland—Liam Redland—had a simple enough task. Through his contact, Evan Brewer, he negotiated a deal with the local contact for the Colombian drug cartel. The drugs purchased were processed and packed for Redland by the Colombians. A percentage was sold in Holland; the rest went farther afield. Across Europe. With the high return for his investment, Redland negotiated a further deal with Brewer, this time for a consignment of weapons. Diel's information mentioned Star Freight. His thoughts were that the company was involved in the shipping of the weapons, hidden in the relief containers they handled for Piet Sonderstrom's charity organization. Once in Chandra the containers could be cleared of the weapons either by looting them on the docks or waiting until they were cleared and then hijacking them.

This time the deal hadn't gone as smoothly.

Charlie Diel had uncovered the details of the network.

Evan Brewer had been exposed as having delivered sensitive weapons stolen from U.S. military stores.

Although Diel's cover had been blown, taking him out of the picture, his compiled information and photographic evidence had been passed to a third party.

It was, Bolan accepted, easy to understand why the bad guys were nervous. Their scheme was under threat of being exposed. Too many things had been turned belly-up in the clear light of day, and secrecy was about to go slithering down the tubes.

The taxi had dropped the warrior on the outskirts of the industrial area. It ran close to the river, an ugly sprawl of service industries serving the main port facilities of Rotterdam. Bolan walked the last quarter of a mile, keeping to the dark spots and the dense shadows.

The night was oily black above the glare of indifferent streetlighting. In the shadows of a closed-down workshop, Bolan had stripped off his outer clothing. Beneath he wore his blacksuit, donned before he had left the hotel. From the carryall he toted, the warrior removed his combat harness and shoulder rig for the Beretta 93-R. The big Desert Eagle was snug in a high-ride holster on his hip, with a Ka-bar combat knife sheathed on the opposite side. Armed with these weapons and the Uzi he had hung on to, Bolan was ready to move on Star Freight. He rolled up his leather jacket, tucked it inside the holdall and hid the bag under some boards lying along the base of the workshop wall.

Star Freight bordered the river itself. The far side of the compound edged a wide strip of dark mud flats regularly washed by the cold waters of the river.

Hunched beneath dripping bushes, Bolan studied the compound beyond the perimeter fence. Vehicles, containers and semitrailers were dotted around the area. There were high stacks of boxes and barrels, piles of truck tires and spare parts. Farther in were the sprawling buildings of the workshops. Lights showed behind grubby windows, and the rainy night sky was lighted by the flashing, high-intensity glare from welding equipment. The clatter of machinery mingled with the throaty roar of diesel engines being revved under test.

Bolan took note of a number of dark figures strolling around the compound. They looked more like guards than regular workers by the way they crossed and recrossed the compound.

He checked out the entrance, a high steel-mesh gate on rollers, watched over by a gateman in a brightly lighted cubicle. Powerful lights on high poles illuminated the gate area.

Bolan worked his way around the compound until he was near the side fence leading down to the river, where he found a section that would have been difficult to cover by the roving guards. Over a long period of time it had been used as a dumping ground for derelict vehicles, abandoned engines and other damaged hardware.

Close to the base of the fence the warrior found a weak spot where the bank had been gradually eroded by the wash of the river at high level. The pressure of the accumulated scrap metal on the other side of the fence had pushed against the chain links and stretched them almost to bursting point. The stressed links had been pushed upward, clearing the soft, muddy ground and leaving a gap. Bolan dropped to the ground, rolled on his back and worked his way under the fence. Once inside the perimeter he eased his way through the scrap pile until he was able to look out across the main compound.

Releasing the Uzi's safety, he made sure the weapon was cocked and ready. The machine pistol held a full magazine, and Bolan carried a spare in one of the blacksuit's zip pockets.

A scrape of sound caught the Executioner's attention. He sank into the deep shadows and watched the approach of one of the figures he had noticed earlier. His initial impression had been correct. The hardman was dressed in dark slacks and a leather jacket, wore a long-peaked cap and carried a stubby Ingram MAC-10.

The sighting of the armed guard gave Bolan's suspicions about the place solid grounding. An honestly run freight company had no reason to employ armed guards. The only reason for the presence of this man was that something illegal was taking place.

Bolan let the guard pass him and vanish from sight. Then he moved swiftly, making his way through an area where numerous trailers were parked. He emerged closer to the workshops than he had expected. Gazing along the length of the building, Bolan spotted an access door about a third of the way along. He cut in the direction of the door, pressing tight against the wall when he reached it.

Aware of the presence of other guards, the warrior didn't hesitate. He checked the door and found it wasn't locked. It opened at his touch. A hum of noise and a splash of light spilled out. Bolan glanced inside and saw that the door led into the workshop beneath a steel structure supporting an upper level. He was able to creep in among the tangle of girders and struts, dusty with age, and observe the activities taking place in the main workshop area.

Although there were a number of vehicles and trailers of varying shape and size scattered about the place, the main interest seemed to be centered around a single container.

It stood on a metal frame, undergoing intense work. From his position Bolan could also see the rear section of the container. Lettering across the aluminum paneling caught his eyes, as did the container's identification number—168.

It was the refrigerated container missing from the dock.

Near the container a long wooden trestle held a number of wooden boxes. They were painted in olive drab and carried stencils Bolan recognized as U.S. military serial numbers. Men clad in coveralls were opening the boxes and removing the contents.

It wasn't difficult to identify the dark shapes of automatic pistols. Another box yielded rapid-fire combat rifles. Smaller, slim metal cases were stacked on the trestle. Ammunition boxes.

Dollies bearing metal drums were wheeled up alongside the container. Each drum was fitted with a pump unit coupled to a flexible hose. Air lines were attached to the pumps and the regulators set. The pump pistons began to stroke with slow deliberation.

A figure dressed in a dark suit appeared. He shouted instructions, waving his arms in anger, and the men gathered around the container broke into action.

Bolan watched with interest as the weapons on the trestle were placed in individual heavy-duty plastic bags, the openings sealed tightly with industrial tape. When fifty of the weapons had been bagged, the man operating the hoses from the metal drums climbed stepladders until they were level with the roof of the container. Valves were opened and the hoses began to pour out a thick, pale brown viscous foam. They appeared to be pumping it inside the container. Bolan realized that they were actually hosing it into the cavity between the container's inner and outer skin. That realization also told him what they were doing.

The two foam materials reacted with each other on contact to swell and fill the cavity with a light honeycomb insulating compound that set within minutes. Once hardened, the foam would help to isolate the container's interior and maintain the low temperatures required to protect the medicines being shipped. The foam-block material was light and could be broken apart by hand, but inside the cavity it maintained a solid formation.

Now, as the foam was steadily built up, the bagged weapons were carried up more ladders and dropped down into the cavity. More foam was applied, and the procedure repeated. The ammunition boxes were also dropped down inside the cavity. More weapons were sealed in plastic and passed up to be dropped into the cavity. The process went on until the foam began to rise above the level of the container side. The equipment was quickly moved around to the other side of the container, out of Bolan's sight, but he could hear the pumps working and watched as more weapons were carried around the container. A man carrying an electric saw dragged steps along the length of the container, leveling off the hardened foam showing above the top of the cavity. Preformed aluminum capping strips were riveted in place, closing off the cavity and completing the operation.

Bolan had to admit it was a clever scheme. Once returned to the dock, the container wouldn't look any different to others lined up with it. Except that in addition to the lifesaving medication stored inside, there was also a cargo designed to do exactly the opposite, a secret cargo of sudden and violent death destined for the already-troubled nation of Chandra.

Unless the Executioner could stop the container from reaching the dock.

Bolan pulled back from his place of concealment, his mind working swiftly as he began to develop a plan of action.

His train of thought was broken as the door he'd used to get inside the workshop was pushed open, and one of the armed guards stood in the opening.

The man's face was taut with concentration, eyes searching the shadows. The look in his eyes told Bolan all he needed to know.

His probe into the compound had been discovered. The how or why didn't matter.

It was more important that Bolan got out. If he didn't the future wouldn't matter.

The Executioner launched himself at the guard. If he could silence the man before he raised any alarm, there might be a chance to break away.

It wasn't to be.

The guard sensed Bolan's presence and turned in his direction. His shouted an alarm, and the muzzle of his MAC-10 arced to line up on Bolan's chest.

8

The Uzi in Bolan's hand stuttered briefly, but the short burst was enough. The slugs chewed into the guard's chest, spinning him sideways. He crashed against the wall, his finger jerking back on the Ingram's trigger. The MAC-10 emptied half its magazine before the dying guard's fingers relaxed and dropped the weapon.

Before the guard had hit the floor, Bolan had stepped around him and was going through the door.

Behind him raised voices were accompanied by the sound of running feet.

The warrior had almost cleared the doorway when a burst of automatic fire echoed wildly from within the workshop area.

The hail of slugs shredded the edge of the doorframe. Bolan felt splinters dig into the shoulder of his blacksuit as he twisted away from the opening, ducking into shadow and bringing the Uzi into play.

The Executioner's keen eye had spotted the gunner's dark outline. The guy was pressed close against a stack of plywood sheets, resting his left arm on the top sheet while he aimed his autoweapon.

Bolan tracked in on the figure and stroked the trigger. The Uzi's rapid burst of 9 mm slugs drilled the gunner in the right side of his chest. The hardman exhaled sharply, unable to even call out. He tumbled backward and hit the concrete with a stunning crash. The back of his skull impacted with enough force to render him unconscious.

In the few seconds afforded him, Bolan had backtracked, covering as much ground as he could before any of the gunner's partners located the source of the shots.

His probe had gone hard in moments, turning a silent examination of the workshop into a threatening situation.

Bolan's mind retraced his route into the complex. He had subconsciously mapped out his escape even as he had entered the place, noting the areas that would lead him into dead ends. His main concern was whether his trail in had been discovered by the enemy. If that was the case, they could easily cut him off, block his escape route and close in.

Somewhere nearby he heard the roar of an engine, followed by the whine of tires burning against concrete. Bolan crouched in the shadow of a half-constructed refrigerator trailer, easing between the heavy wheels.

He saw the dancing twin beams of headlights moving through the yard, zigzagging as the vehicle rolled around the parked trucks and trailers. Now he could pick out raised voices, men calling to each other. The sound of running footsteps echoed between the stacks of building materials.

He heard someone approaching from his rear. His instinct had been correct. They were moving in from all directions, the idea being to surround him.

The probing vehicle came into view, rounding a set of metal racks. It braked, rocking on its springs. Bolan recognized an open-backed 4x4. Standing inside the open bed were two armed men. A third sat beside the driver.

The 4x4 stood between Bolan and the unknown number of men closing in at his back. He slid farther under the chassis of the trailer, peering out the other side. Figures moved back and forth in the near distance.

The warrior took a gamble that the group he was watching now were the least organized. They were hampered by the fact they were moving through a collection of damaged vehicles parked in an untidy sprawl. In among the vehicles were surplus items of machinery, old tires and abandoned axles. There was no direct way through, forcing the searchers to angle back and forth.

Bolan heard the rumble of the 4x4 as the driver teased the gas pedal. The other group was closing in fast, too.

He made his decision and acted on it.

Rolling clear of the trailer, the warrior crouched and ran into the vehicle graveyard, ducking under a trailer chassis as he spotted one of the searchers moving his way.

He might have got away with it if one of the men in the 4x4 hadn't decided to switch on a spotlight at that moment and play it over the area Bolan had just entered.

For a brief second the Executioner was caught in the white pool of light. A man yelled, pointing, and moments later the yard erupted to a concentrated burst of fire. Bullets peppered the aluminum side of the trailer Bolan was beneath, forcing him to drop to his knees. He didn't remain where he was for long, knowing that sooner or later one of those bullets was going to find him. He crawled forward until he reached the far end of the trailer, hugging the double set of wheels.

Hardmen were converging on his hiding place, calling orders to one another. They were all trying to direct the rest. No one listened.

Bolan took advantage of the momentary chaos. He leaned out from his hiding place and triggered the Uzi. The harsh crackle of the weapon was followed by a scream of pain as the stream of 9 mm rounds shattered a man's legs and dumped him on the ground. Confusion reigned as the other searchers scattered, tumbling over dark objects in their haste to get away from the autofire. He caught one more before they vanished, stitching the guy from waist to throat. The hardman crashed into an old engine, dropping his weapon as he arched over the block of rusting metal, his blood already leaking from chest wounds.

Breaking clear of the trailer, the Executioner moved deeper into the jumble of vehicles. At his back the shouting increased. The distant rumble of the 4x4 turned to a full-throated roar as the driver hit the gas. He began to circle the scrap area, the spotlight probing the deep shadows, seeking Bolan as he wormed his way through the vehicles.

A gunner burst into view yards ahead of Bolan, yelling that he had found the intruder and swinging around his weapon to pick up the Executioner. The man's priorities bought him nothing but grief. Instead of concentrating on Bolan, the guy tried to call in his partners *and* trigger his weapon at the same time. He was a fraction slow on both counts. Bolan's Uzi chattered briefly, but with devastating effect, the volley of 9 mm bullets slicing into the guy's throat. He twisted and crashed headlong into the side of a trailer body before slithering ungraciously to the ground.

The Uzi had locked on an empty breech. Bolan discarded the used magazine. He pulled his remaining clip from his blacksuit pocket and clicked it in place, then snapped back the cocking bolt.

Catching movement on his left, Bolan dropped into a combat crouch, sweeping the Uzi around to pick out the armed man confronting him. The gunner fired first, letting loose with an uncoordinated burst that blew ragged holes in the aluminum panels of the trailer next to Bolan. The Executioner returned fire, placing his shots with accuracy and driving the stunned gunner backward. The guy let out a long moan as he was doubled over by the force of the slugs drilling into his body. He dropped to the ground and lay shuddering in a pool of oil.

Moving on quickly, Bolan used the parked vehicles as cover and staging posts, pausing briefly to check ahead before making his next jump. Keeping to the deepest patches of shadow, the Executioner remained as elusive as he could, only engaging the enemy when there was no other way out of a situation. His priority was to reach the perimeter fence before he found himself surrounded and cut off.

He finally reached the edge of the parking area. The compound lay open and exposed between himself and the fence. Bolan crouched in the darkness under the chassis of a rusting trailer. He had pinpointed his place of entry. All he had to do was reach it.

The warrior tensed his muscles, then pushed out from under the chassis. He headed directly for the spot in the fence where he had entered the compound. The only difference now was that an armed man stood close to the spot.

The gunner snapped to attention when he saw Bolan heading his way. He fired off a burst, the slugs clanging off metal to Bolan's left. The Executioner, dropping to a crouch, leveled the Uzi, aimed and fired. His short blast took the guy in the upper chest, flinging him back against the fence. The stricken gunner was catapulted off the wire, falling facedown on the damp earth.

Bolan pushed upright and kept running.

He was more than halfway across the open ground when the 4x4 swung into view from behind a pile of truck tires. It swerved in his direction. Above the roar of the engine, Bolan picked up the chatter of autoweapons. Bullets ate into the soft earth at his feet as he weaved from side to side, presenting a target constantly changing direction. The strategy seemed to be working until the warrior felt the burning sting of a bullet across the back of his left calf.

The fence was still yards away, and he was going to have to pause long enough to get through it. For certain the gunners in the 4x4 weren't about to grant him any free time.

Bolan about-faced without warning, bringing up the Uzi. He triggered a long burst at the windshield, saw the glass shatter and then the vehicle lurched to the right, almost turning over. One of the gunners in the rear lost his grip. He went over the side, screaming, and smashed facedown on the ground, his limp body bouncing for yards before coming to rest. The other man in the rear of the vehicle managed to hang on, but he was unable to place any accurate fire because of the 4x4's erratic course.

Tracking the vehicle, Bolan aimed for one of the front tires. The Uzi snapped out a burst, 9 mm slugs shredding the rubber. The tire blew, and the 4x4 dipped as the steel rim dropped to the concrete. It twisted in the opposite direction with such force that it rolled, crashed on its side and skidded along the ground some distance before coming to a rest.

The surviving gunner stumbled from the wreck, hauling his trailing SMG around to confront Bolan. The Executioner triggered his own weapon, catching the guy in the lower body and driving him to the ground in a bloody jumble of limbs.

Bolan raked the exposed fuel tank with 9 mm slugs. Gasoline began to jet from the ragged holes, spreading across the ground. A second burst, which emptied the magazine, threw a brief spray of sparks into the rising vapor fumes. The resultant gush of flame spread rapidly, filling the air and racing across the ground.

The flame created a temporary wall between Bolan and his pursuers.

The warrior threw the empty Uzi aside and drew the Desert Eagle as he reached the fence. He kicked at the loose section to widen the gap and wriggled through, sliding down the grassy bank to the service road below. He kept moving, heading away from the compound and the glare of flames from the burning 4x4. He paused at the deserted workshop and picked up the carryall. Slipping into the leather jacket, Bolan made for the main highway that skirted the industrial area.

Behind him, over the compound of the freight yard, the night sky was bathed in glowing orange and the darker gray of oily smoke.

Whatever else he had achieved, Bolan decided, he had at least verified that Charlie Diel's information had been correct. While he hadn't managed to physically destroy the weapons consignment, he had left the enemy with the knowledge that someone was onto their game.

9

The pale light of early dawn was beginning to streak
the misty sky as the cab dropped Bolan around the
corner from the hotel. Making his silent way to the
rear of the building, the Executioner used the kitchen
entrance to get inside. At this time of night there was
only a cleaner on duty, mopping the floor around the
stoves. Bolan waited until the woman's back was
turned, then eased through the kitchen, emerging in
the silent, gloomy restaurant. He made his way from
there along the corridor that led to the back stairs,
then up to the floor where the room was located.

A sixth sense told Bolan to move with caution.
Something felt wrong. Pulling the Beretta, he placed
the carryall in an alcove before approaching the room.
He paused at the door, pressing his ear to the panel.
He couldn't hear any sound from inside. It was possible that Kelly was resting. He eased back from the
door, peering at the bottom gap. Light showed underneath. As Bolan watched, a shadow passed from one
side of the door to the other.

The warrior tapped on the door after stepping to
one side. There was a faint rustle of sound, then the
shadow moved again.

"Kelly, it's Mike. Open up."

He waited. Moments later the catch was released and the door opened a fraction.

Bolan tensed. He knew now that it wasn't Kelly on the other side of the door. She would have answered him, made some remark. It would have been against the woman's nature not to have spoken. Bolan had learned that much from being in her company.

He moved quickly then, slamming the sole of his left boot against the door and driving it open with terrific force. As the door flew open, Bolan went in fast and low, ducking to his right and rolling.

He heard a man grunt in pain. There was the thump of something hard hitting the carpeted floor; probably a weapon. As Bolan regained his feet and started to rise, he heard the door slam shut behind him.

He registered that the room was only partially lighted, illuminated by the soft lamp fixed to the wall above the bed. He spotted a dark shape scrambling off the mattress, the metal barrel of a handgun catching the subdued light. The gun began to swing in Bolan's direction.

He didn't hesitate. His finger stroked the 93-R's trigger, and a suppressed trio of 9 mm tumblers hissed from the muzzle. The rising figure was punched off the bed and driven into the corner of the room. The shot man had time for a brief grunt of pain before he crumpled to the floor.

The Executioner whirled, aware of the second figure looming behind him. The man hadn't had time to find his fallen weapon, so he rushed at Bolan with arms outstretched, fingers clawing at the warrior's face. Bolan pulled his head aside, sweeping the Beretta's steel in a swift arc. The autopistol slammed against the guy's skull, driving him to his knees. Bolan followed through with a second blow that whacked the stunned man across the back of the head. He flopped facedown on the carpet, moaning softly, and didn't try to get up.

Turning, the warrior moved to the door and locked it. He flipped on the main light and quickly scanned the room. He knew even before he looked that Kelly McBride was missing.

The man in the far corner was already dead, his chest slick with blood.

Bolan crouched beside the other man, who was beginning to stir. There was a smear of bright blood on his face where Bolan had hit him. Flipping the guy over on his back, Bolan stripped off the man's belt and used it to strap his hands together. He grabbed a handful of shirt and dumped him in the room's easy chair. Then he sat on the edge of the bed and waited for the man to come around.

When he did, Bolan let him see the Beretta. He tracked the muzzle in on his adversary's head and held it steady.

"You understand English?" Bolan asked.

The man nodded, blinking his eyes to clear them.

"You understand it well enough to know I'm ready to kill you if I don't get the answers I need?"

The man looked beyond Bolan to where his former partner lay. The look in his eyes told Bolan he understood well enough.

"Where's the woman?"

Oddly the man laughed, a short, derisive sound.

"Where you won't find her," the man replied, his Dutch accent was heavy and slow.

"I'm not all that impressed by your friends' hospitality or manners. Maybe I'll do something about it— starting with you."

The Dutchman smiled. "You're a damn fool to think you can just walk in and push us around. You know who you are dealing with?"

"A bunch of local hoods is all I see."

"You are wrong, Yank. My people run this town. We supply all the drugs in this area. We have contacts all over Rotterdam. You won't get away with this, I promise."

"What is it I'm supposed to be doing?"

"We don't like your involvement. We'll take care of the Colombians. All you are doing is getting in the way."

Bolan considered the man's statement. The Dutchman seemed to be implying that he was interfering with some localized war between drug gangs. Perhaps he was. But only by proxy. His contact with the parties involved had come about by circumstance rather than deliberate intent. Bolan had no regrets over that. If a few of the drug pushers and dealers walked into his line of fire, the warrior wasn't going to lose much sleep over them. Part of his ongoing war was with the worldwide drug fraternity, so any who found themselves under the Executioner's gun during his current forays were going to pay the price of their ugly business.

"Why have you taken the woman?" Bolan asked.

"Insurance. You back away and maybe we let her live. Stay out of our business unless you want her dead. It's an easy decision."

"Wrong," Bolan told him. "I don't cave in to threats, and I don't like blackmailers."

The Dutchman shrugged. "Then she's going to die. I promise you that. And so will that damn Englishman, Brewer. With luck I'll be there when they drop the hammer on you, too."

"More threats?"

"It's a tough world. Like I said, we don't play games." As soon as the words left the man's mouth, he made a move toward his hideaway gun.

The warrior shifted the Beretta's muzzle and pulled the trigger.

Bolan stepped away from the dead man and holstered the Beretta. The game had played him another wild card, in the shape of the local Rotterdam drug traffickers. Somehow they had dealt themselves in, deciding to involve Bolan and McBride in their vendetta against Evan Brewer and the Colombians. It could easily have become confusing, the warrior admitted to himself. But there was one thing that was very clear in his mind. The locals might have dealt themselves into the game, but it would be the Executioner who canceled their play.

He pulled out Charlie Diel's package and examined the details on Evan Brewer. According to Diel the Briton, though based in Rotterdam, didn't maintain a permanent base. It wasn't surprising the way he seemed to operate. Brewer's shady dealings, and his current fallout with the Dutch drug dealers in preference to the Colombians, suggested he was walking a thin wire that might snap at any moment. Bolan didn't care much for the man's problems. Brewer was reaping what he had sown. But he *might* have a line on where the Dutch drug dealers were holding Kelly.

Bolan located a telephone number Diel had jotted down. The undercover agent had recorded the number as an emergency contact. As far as the Executioner was concerned, this was an emergency.

He picked up the phone and punched the number for an outside line. Then he keyed in the number and waited as it rang.

A woman's voice answered in Dutch.

"I speak only English," Bolan stated. "I need to contact Evan Brewer. It's important."

The woman hesitated, then Bolan heard her speaking softly to someone.

"Yes?"

This time the voice belonged to a man. The accent was British.

"Brewer? We need to talk and fast."

"Says who?"

"Call me Mike. I'm on Charlie Diel's team. He's out of the game and right now, Brewer, you're a marked man."

"Meaning?"

"There are some locals who want your head. They don't like your dealings with the Colombians. I've just had a run in with a couple of them, and their message was clear. They have a hit list with your name at the top."

"How do I know I can trust you?" Brewer asked.

"You decide on that. All I can say is don't take too long because the pair I dealt with are going to have friends."

The man on the other end of the line cursed softly. He muttered to himself, then came back to Bolan.

"Take this address down," Brewer said. He rattled off the location. "I'll be there in thirty minutes. I'll wait another half hour, then I'm gone. And I'll have a gun, so I hope you're playing this straight."

"Brewer, keep your eyes open. The locals have better sources than I do. They're already tracking you, and talking isn't on their agenda."

Bolan cut the connection. He stood for a moment, considering what he was about to do.

Whatever the cost, he had to follow it through. Kelly's safety was important to him. She had been dragged into his business, and there was no way Bolan could abandon her.

10

Bolan parked the Mercedes around the corner from the dilapidated apartment building where he was to meet Evan Brewer, and sat for a minute, checking the Beretta and studying the area. It was in a gloomy, run-down section of the city, not far from the waterfront, the sort of area where people minded their own business. The warrior could see why Brewer used it as a bolthole.

The Executioner still wore his blacksuit, with his leather jacket over it to conceal his shoulder rig. He knew he risked drawing attention to himself dressed in his combat gear, but he had no choice. Luckily, as it was still early, the streets were deserted.

He had found the keys to the Mercedes on one of the drug traffickers he had left in the hotel. The car itself was parked along the street, tucked away behind a delivery truck. Bolan had tried the key in the door and it had worked. Almost-new expensive Mercedeses weren't the kind of vehicle normally found parked in such an area. Bolan had searched the trunk and interior, but hadn't come up with anything to identify the owner.

Now he sat staring through the windshield, the wipers snaking back and forth in front of his eyes, checking out the building.

Was Brewer waiting up there alone, or had the traffickers already found him? Only one way to find out, Bolan decided, and exited the Mercedes. He crossed the wet street, wondering idly if it was ever going to stop raining in Holland.

Keeping to the shadows, he checked the alley running the length of the building. Partway along was a Mercedes that could have been a twin to the one he had appropriated. Only this time there was a dark figure sitting behind the wheel.

Bolan hugged the grimy wall, closing in on the silent vehicle. The wheelman, chewing on a thick cigar that had almost filled the interior with smoke, was totally unaware of the black-clad figure. The warrior had the driver's door open and the muzzle of the 93-R jammed into the guy's neck before he could catch his breath.

Pulling the driver out, Bolan checked him for weapons. There was a 9 mm Browning BDA autopistol sheathed under the man's left arm. The Executioner dropped the magazine and lost the weapon in the darkness of the alley.

"English?" he asked.

The man shook his head.

Bolan reached inside and took the keys from the ignition. He shoved the man toward the rear of the car, unlocked the trunk and indicated he wanted the man to climb inside—which provoked an immediate, violent reaction.

The wheelman spun, snatching the cigar from his mouth and jabbing it at Bolan's face. As the warrior pulled back, the man lunged forward, a growl of rage bursting from his lips. His thick hands clawed at his adversary's throat, catching briefly, then slipping as Bolan ducked. He came in under the outstretched arms, hammering his left shoulder deep into the exposed midsection. The wheelman coughed as the breath was forced from his lungs. He arched back, colliding with the rear end of the Mercedes.

Still bent over, Bolan uncoiled, whipping the Beretta around and slamming it against the side of the wheelman's skull. The guy's legs caved and he slumped to the ground.

The Executioner holstered the Beretta, then caught hold of the unconscious man and heaved him into the trunk, slamming the lid shut. He threw the keys into a trash can and retraced his steps down the alley.

He crossed the sidewalk and entered the dimly lighted lobby of the apartment building, keeping his eyes open for any lookouts. The interior was deserted. Bolan eased the Beretta into his hand, keeping the autopistol pressed against his leg as he climbed the stairs.

He reached the third floor without incident. Moving along the grubby, uncarpeted passage, Bolan paused at the door to Brewer's apartment.

He tensed as he heard a sudden scraping sound from inside, which was followed by a soft thud and the sound of a man groaning in pain. Subdued voices reached his ears. There was the sound of a blow, then another.

Bolan put his shoulder to the door and heaved. The door gave a fraction. He drew back and hit it again, harder. On the inside, wood cracked and the door flew open, crashing against the inside wall.

The room was partially lighted by a single lamp, which gave enough light for Bolan to recognize Evan Brewer's profile from one of Charlie Diel's photographs. The slim Briton was at a window, struggling with the stiff latch, swearing angrily.

The warrior sprinted across the room and dropped a big hand on Brewer's bony shoulder, pulling him back from the window.

"You don't understand," Brewer yelled. His face was beaded with sweat, and there was fresh blood and bruises on the narrow line of his jaw.

Floorboards creaked.

Bolan turned away from Brewer and caught a shadow of movement lunging in from behind.

The blow aimed for the Executioner's skull caught Brewer across the left shoulder, knocking him against the jammed window. The pane of glass cracked, and he sagged over the sill.

Bolan completed his turn, coming face-to-face with the guy who had emerged from the shadows. He was a tall man, with a thin, sallow face. Hard, small eyes stared at the warrior with unconcealed animosity. The guy swung again, missing as Bolan drifted away from the fist. The guy stepped back as the warrior straightened. When he moved again it was to swing up his right foot in a swift snap-kick that took the Beretta out of Bolan's hand. The gun spun across the room, thumping against the carpet.

The hardman gave a self-satisfied grunt and lunged at Bolan again.

Brewer, bleeding from numerous glass cuts, slumped to his knees below the window, his eyes searching the floor.

Bolan studied his adversary as he began to move in, aware now he was dealing with someone with more than a brawler's knowledge.

The hardman tensed, coming in fast, faking a fist movement then bringing his lethal snap-kick into play.

The Executioner dropped to the floor, under the kick. He employed a sweep with his own leg, knocking his opponent's foot off the floor.

The man went down, breaking his fall, but not fast enough to avoid Bolan's attack. The warrior was already moving, his left arm snaking around his adversary's neck, his right following to complete the grip. As the hardman began to struggle, Bolan put on the pressure, twisting sharply. The man's neck snapped with a soft pop.

Brewer had located the Beretta. He shoved himself to his feet and went after the weapon.

Pushing aside the corpse, Bolan lunged after Brewer. He reached him as the Briton bent to retrieve the 93-R, slamming bodily into the bending figure. Brewer was hurled into the wall. Bolan scooped up the Beretta and loomed over the groaning figure. He pressed the cold steel of the 93-R's muzzle against Brewer's forehead.

"You owe me," Bolan growled. "I just stopped that guy from killing you."

"Yeah?" Brewer touched a hand to his bleeding nose. "Hope it ain't bloody well broken," he complained. He stared at Bolan. "You Mike?"

Bolan nodded.

"I should have guessed. What do you mean I *owe* you? What do you want, a bleedin' big kiss and a hug?"

"I'll settle for a location."

"What the hell are you on about?"

"Your onetime friends have something I need back. Where would they take an item they don't want found? Where they wouldn't be disturbed while they asked questions?"

Brewer grinned. "Hang on. I'm supposed to be the one getting the help. What do I get out of this deal?"

"How about I let you stay alive?"

The words sank in. Brewer glanced beyond Bolan to the dead man stretched out on the carpet. He had died too quickly and too easily.

"Trouble with these Dutch buggers is they don't give a guy the opportunity to negotiate. The Colombians made me a better offer. So I took it. Okay, so I owed them money. I was going to come to an arrangement. Would they listen? Hell, no. All they could think about was killing me and then taking on the Colombians."

Bolan eased off. He moved across the room and closed the door. The Beretta remained trained on the Briton.

"Are you serious about killing me, as well?"

"I don't like what you do, Brewer. You trade in wholesale slaughter. You sell death just to make a dollar."

"It's a business that's been around a long time."

"That doesn't justify it. And lately you've been handling stolen weapons. Some from U.S. military bases. If you get picked up for that, my offer will start to sound interesting."

"Do me a favor. I'm too far gone to be upset by any 'death before dishonor' crap. You know as well as I do that all the industrial nations are in the arms business up to their necks. Some of my best customers are government agencies."

"Right now is all that bothers me. And I don't play by government rules. If I decide you die, there's no vote on it."

"Yeah, yeah. The picture's clear. You're a harder bastard to deal with than Diel."

"Keep that in mind. Charlie Diel got himself involved in something deeper than he'd expected."

"Is he dead?"

"I'd be surprised if he wasn't by now."

Brewer lowered his head into his hands.

"God, how do I walk away from this one? The way it's going, every hard case in Holland wants me dead."

"Then do yourself a favor, Brewer. Give me what I want and you can take off."

Brewer sleeved blood from his chin.

"Damned if I do, damned if I don't. Do I have a choice?"

"No. But you can count on one thing."

Brewer raised a quizzical eyebrow. "What?"

"I keep my word."

"Bloody funny, but I believe you."

Brewer crossed the room on still-shaky legs. He pushed open the bathroom door, bending over the basin to sluice the blood away from his face. He dabbed it dry on a towel that rapidly became bloodstained. Raising his eyes, he stared at his reflection in the mirror.

"Right bloody mess I look."

Bolan came to stand in the bathroom doorway.

"Okay," Brewer said, holding up his hands. "I'm giving you my best guess on this. There's a boat yard upriver. In an estuary."

Returning to the living room, he searched for a sheet of paper and began to sketch a crude map. "There's a sixty-foot seagoing cruiser moored there called the *Dark Runner*. It belongs to the Rotterdam syndicate. I know they've used it before for *meetings*. If they need privacy it could be the place you're looking for."

The warrior took the paper and pocketed it. He turned and headed for the door, single-minded in his purpose now.

"Hey, what about me?" Brewer called out.

Bolan paused. "You've got a stay of execution."

"Dependent on what?"

"Whether you've told me the truth," Bolan said with chilling finality.

11

Although dawn was starting to lighten the sky, thick banks of fog had moved up the estuary, cloaking the boat yard. Rolling banks of the gray-white mist hovered just above ground level. The persistent rain had slackened to a fine drizzle.

Mack Bolan hunched in the shadow of a rusting steel barge that had been hauled out of the water. Rain ran down the corroding metal sides and dripped onto his back. The Beretta 93-R nestled in its shoulder rig. The Desert Eagle was cradled in the crook of his left arm while he studied the lay of the land. His surveillance of the yard also gave him a brief opportunity to snatch moments of the rest that had been denied him during the endless night since his arrival.

The conditions of his ongoing skirmishes reminded Bolan of his time in Vietnam, when it had been commonplace for missions to roll on relentlessly. The East Asia war zone allowed no concessions—there were no rest breaks, or time out because a firefight or patrol had been ongoing for hours. Then, as now, time meant nothing during combat. It was strike and strike again, moving from one point to the next, with little time for anything other than reloading. The warrior gave little thought to his own comfort, except for when it came to snatching a few moments respite during a lull in the hostilities.

Brewer's directions had led him to the boat yard without difficulty. The gates had been closed and barred, so he'd had to climb over. The whole yard looked as if it had been shut down for a time. It had a deserted, almost-abandoned look to it. The untidy sprawl of wooden buildings rose above a span of mud flats that preceded the estuary itself. A collection of boats in various stages of repair or abandonment straggled along the flats. Farther out were wooden quays that jutted into deep water. The few craft moored there were covered with tarpaulins, dark and empty.

At the farthermost berth sat the 60-foot cruiser, *Dark Runner,* that Evan Brewer had described to Bolan. Through the fog he could make out the soft glow of lights inside the aft cabin. He also picked out two men, fore and aft, who were on watch.

At the landward end of the quay, Bolan spotted a number of parked vehicles. His own was hidden a quarter mile back.

Once inside the yard the warrior had worked his way along the water's edge, using the boats as cover until he had reached his present location.

He sat now, watching the cruiser. His observations had identified only the two men on watch. He hadn't seen anyone on land. Even so, Bolan took his time, allowing a good half hour to slip by before he moved.

The easy part was reaching the quay. He slipped beneath it, easing in between the wooden posts that supported the walkway, his feet sinking into the soft mud. Using the underside of the planked walkway, Bolan moved out along the quay. After ten feet he was in water. It became deeper as he edged farther out, and well before he reached the end of the quay he was off the bottom, floating in the gentle swell of the cold water, pulling himself along by the wooden pilings.

The smooth, white-painted hull rose and fell in front of him. He pushed away from the quay and swam the length of the cruiser until he reached the stern. A thick rope snaked from the boat to a mooring piling on the quay. The warrior reached up, grasped the coarse line and hauled himself from the water, hooking his legs over the rope. He slipped the Desert Eagle back in its holster, so both hands were free. Then he worked his way up the rope, grasping the metal rim of the rail, and peered through to get a view of the deck.

The man on watch at the stern had his back to Bolan. The Executioner saw the telltale webbing of a sling over the man's shoulder, with the butt end of a subgun protruding from beneath the guy's arm.

Easing over the rail, Bolan catfooted up behind the lookout. He allowed the guy to wander to the far rail and stare out over the dark spread of water, then slipped in behind him.

The warrior's right arm snaked over the sentry's shoulder and across his neck, the top of his hand under the exposed chin. He hooked his fingers and pulled back sharply, pushing his right hip into the base of the spine and his right shoulder against the base of the skull. The action put instant pressure on the man's spine and also cut off his air supply. The sentry began to struggle. Bolan leaned back hard, increasing the pressure, and the guard slipped into a painless death. The Executioner placed him on the deck, then dragged him into the shadows of a deck hatch. He relieved the guy of his subgun, sliding it out of sight.

Bolan moved the length of the deck, staying low and watching for anyone emerging from below. He paused to locate the second guard. This one had decided to relax. He had leaned his autoweapon against the side rail while he lighted a cigarette. He had time for one draw before the warrior took him with the same stranglehold he'd used on the first guard. With a lung full of smoke the guy died quickly, sagging in Bolan's arms.

The warrior fisted his newly acquired subgun and ran a swift check on the weapon, which was a Heckler & Koch MP-5. The rapid-fire weapon was fitted with a 30-round magazine. Bolan eased off the safety, then turned and crept in the direction of the hatch leading below deck.

The main cabin lay at the stern of the cruiser. Bolan, moving with extreme caution, ears and eyes alert for any warning signs, headed along the central passage.

The interior of the cruiser was luxurious. The deck under his feet was thickly carpeted, deadening any sound he might have made. As he neared the main cabin, he picked up the murmur of voices behind a pair of double doors. There was the clink of glasses, laughter, then a voice Bolan recognized—tinged with an edge of fear.

It was Kelly McBride.

Bolan didn't hesitate. He launched a powerhouse kick that burst the doors open and went in fast and low, the MP-5 tracking ahead of him.

There were eight people in the cabin, and two of them died within seconds of Bolan's entry.

The first hardman was armed with a stubby Ingram, hanging from his thick wrist by a strap. The guy died trying to bring the weapon into play as Bolan's H&K pumped out a short burst. The hot 9 mm slugs burned into the guy's broad torso, spinning him in a bloody half circle. He collided with a drinks trolley, scattering bottles and glasses across the carpeted floor.

While the hardman was on the way to the floor, Bolan had picked up a second gunner, slipping off a high stool and grabbing his own Ingram from the polished bar counter. The guy, off to the warrior's right, opened fire, the prolonged burst from the MAC-10 chewing ragged holes in the wood-veneer paneling on the cabin walls to one side of the doors. Dropping to a low crouch, Bolan angled the MP-5 up at the gunner, touching the trigger and sending a quick burst into his chest. The hardman fell back against the bar, dropping his Ingram so that he could claw at his bloody chest.

A suited figure dropped the glass he was holding and lunged at the Executioner. He was only feet away, and his looping right grazed Bolan's jaw. Letting the guy's momentum pull him in close, Bolan, still gripping the MP-5, delivered a powerful elbow smash to the side of his attacker's face. The brutal impact broke the guy's jaw and drove him to the floor, where he lay moaning and clutching at his injured face.

Bolan put his back to the wall, covering the cabin with the MP-5.

"Hands where I can see them," he snapped, laying the muzzle of the subgun on the three remaining figures. "Do it now, or die. Simple as that."

Kelly McBride and Jan Wender were seated to one side of the trio, tied up. Wender's face was a bruised and bloody mass. His shirt had been ripped open, and two long gashes oozed blood down his chest.

McBride had a large bruise on the left side of her face. Other than that she appeared unharmed.

"Any more on board?" Bolan asked.

"Just the two on deck," one of the men answered, his tone sullen.

"We can forget about them," Bolan said. "I want to see all your weapons on the floor. Now!"

The Executioner watched the three closely, ready to react if anyone made a hero play. It wouldn't have been the first time a man under threat from a gun decided he was faster. Pride, bravado, pure stupidity—call it by any name—but there was always the chance someone might figure he could beat the odds. Most of those were dead now. Proof that they hadn't been faster. This time Bolan was facing a trio who appeared to be using their brains. He saw three handguns drop to the carpeted floor of the cabin, to be followed by a pair of knives.

"You," he said to the man who had spoken before. "I want my friends untied."

While McBride and Wender were being freed, Bolan gestured to the two other men.

"Over by the bar. Sit with your backs against it. Hands on the top of your heads."

As soon as McBride and Wender were free, Bolan ordered the third man to join his partners.

"Can you make it out of here?"

McBride nodded. The fear he'd seen in her eyes had receded now, and she had regained control of her emotions.

"What's been happening, Mike? It's like some crazy nightmare."

"Mdofa's people have been dealing with the Dutch branch of the Colombian cartel. Drugs for cash, cash for weapons and the weapons intended for Mdofa's overthrow of the legal government in Chandra."

"How did you find us?"

"Evan Brewer. There were a couple of local heavies waiting in the hotel room when I got back. I found out they had you and what they intended doing if I didn't back off. So I needed to find out where you were. Brewer had dealings with the local traffickers before their fallout. So I appealed to his better nature and he gave me this location."

McBride indicated the silent traffickers. "They said not to expect you. Or Brewer."

"They had their shots and missed," Bolan explained simply.

"Mike, how did they find out where we were staying?"

Bolan turned to the three traffickers.

"I'm interested in that question myself," he said.

One of the traffickers smiled. "We were given information," he admitted, "from an interested but unknown party."

The warrior's curiosity was aroused. Who would be charitable enough to give the Rotterdam traffickers helpful information? The answer eluded him, so he put the matter to the back of his mind for the time being.

"Did you find what you were looking for at the freight company?"

Bolan nodded. "The missing container and the weapons. But I had to get out when the natives became restless."

McBride didn't pursue the matter further. She knew what Bolan was saying.

"What happened to Jan?" Bolan asked.

"He was picked up when he tried to move my car."

The Dutchman shrugged apologetically. "I should have listened to what you said, Mr. Belasko. I thought I was helping. If Kelly's car couldn't be pinpointed, it might have helped delay you being traced."

"How did you end up here?" Bolan asked. "The guys chasing us in Amsterdam were Redland's."

"I was snatched soon after I left in Kelly's car. Then the car I was forced into was hit itself. I was tied up and blindfolded. I ended up here."

"Jan was here when they brought me on board. You can see what they did to him."

"Sorry I didn't get here sooner."

"Do we owe Brewer thanks, or did he point the finger because you forced him to?"

"Brewer was in a vindictive frame of mind after his ex-buddies tried to retire him. We made a deal. I agreed to let him walk if he pointed me in the direction of the local mob's safehouse."

"So what do we do now?" McBride asked.

Before Bolan could frame a reply, there was a sudden flurry of movement in the direction of the three traffickers by the bar. One of them lunged forward, rolled across the carpeted floor and reached for one of the discarded Ingrams. It was the man with the broken jaw.

Bolan pushed McBride aside and brought up the MP-5.

Jan Wender caught hold of her, dragging her clear of the warrior's field of fire.

Rising on one knee, the drug trafficker swept up the Ingram, his finger stroking the trigger. The lethal weapon spewed out a stream of fire that cut a deadly swath across the cabin.

McBride, pushed off balance, fell to her knees. Wender, his body half-turned as he shoved the woman clear, caught the Ingram's blast in his upper back and skull. He was thrown forward, erupting blood, and tumbled to the floor in a lifeless sprawl.

The MP-5 tracked the gunner, and Bolan touched the trigger, laying down a sharp burst that tore into the guy's chest and throat. The trafficker flopped over, arms wide, his face registering shock and surprise.

The warrior's peripheral vision caught a glimpse of more movement. He turned, picking up the other two traffickers as they scrambled toward their weapons. He didn't hesitate. The MP-5 caught the pair before they were upright, and Bolan emptied the magazine into them. The traffickers tumbled across the carpet, dappling it with their blood.

Bolan tossed aside the empty subgun and pulled out the Desert Eagle.

McBride was on her knees beside her friend's body. She glanced up as Bolan held out a hand to her.

"I can't believe they killed him, Mike," she said in a choked voice. "They didn't have to."

"They didn't have to go into the drug business, either, but they did. Now let's get off this sinking ship."

The woman frowned. "Sinking? We're not sinking."

"Give it time."

TIME STRETCHED to ten minutes. McBride stood on the quay waiting for Bolan, who had returned to the cruiser. When he finally appeared, he joined her and led her away from the water.

"I've got a car," he said. "This way."

"What were you doing back there?" McBride asked.

"Look," Bolan said.

The vessel was lowering into the water, by the stern. Bubbles rose to the surface, bursting instantly.

"I opened the sea cocks," Bolan explained.

"Is that all?"

Before the warrior could answer there was a brilliant flash, followed by a solid explosion that opened a ragged hole in the cruiser's sides, aft of the wheelhouse. As debris flew in all directions, a secondary explosion filled the night sky with flame and smoke.

A mushrooming ball of searing fire hurled fiery tendrils across the water and over the shore.

"*That*'s all," Bolan replied.

They had almost cleared the boat yard's buildings when two cars rolled out of the darkness, their headlights suddenly flashing on. The cars pulled to a stop yards away from Bolan and his companion.

The Executioner touched McBride's arm, easing her to one side. He held the Desert Eagle in readiness, and wondered who he would be facing this time around.

12

The passenger door opened on the lead vehicle, a Volvo sedan, and a man climbed out. He advanced into the circle of light cast by the car headlights. When he reached Bolan he glanced at the gun in the Executioner's hand and smiled benignly.

"Mike Belasko, I presume. My name is Franz Van Hooten. I'm an inspector with the Rotterdam drug squad, and though we probably would not have handled the situation in the same manner, I suppose we should be grateful for your assistance. We've had these drug traffickers under surveillance for some time."

Bolan studied the beefy Dutchman. Van Hooten wore a trilby hat and a thick overcoat against the ceaseless drizzle. The two men who had followed him from the parked cars were similarly dressed.

"You have ID?" the Executioner asked brusquely.

Van Hooten nodded. "Of course." The inspector produced a small leather wallet from his pocket, handed it to Bolan and watched as the American examined the contents.

"It says you're Franz Van Hooten." He passed the wallet to McBride.

"Looks very much like other police ID I've seen," she stated as she handed it back to Van Hooten.

"My men will show you theirs if you wish."

Bolan waved the offer aside. He eased the Desert Eagle back into its holster. "All we want, Inspector, is a chance to get into some dry clothes. And I need to get to a telephone."

Van Hooten turned to his two waiting officers and spoke to them in Dutch.

"He's telling them to radio for additional help so he can get us to safety," McBride translated.

"Please," Van Hooten said, indicating his waiting car.

The Executioner took his companion's arm and led her to the vehicle. He opened the rear door and helped her inside, then entered. Van Hooten eased himself in alongside Bolan and pulled the door shut. He leaned forward and spoke to the waiting driver, who nodded. One of Van Hooten's officers slipped into the other front seat.

The Volvo rolled forward, completing a wide circle that took it back toward the access road. The second police car fell in behind them. The small convoy reached the main road and picked up speed.

"What exactly is your involvement in all this, Inspector?" Bolan asked.

"My principals are concerned that matters have been getting out of hand, Mr. Belasko. As a policeman, my task is to see that those concerns are laid to rest. We are all looking for a peaceful life. Don't you agree?"

Bolan didn't answer. He was watching the empty streets speed by as the police car accelerated. His combat sense was flaring to life. He wasn't certain why, but he didn't trust Van Hooten.

"Inspector," McBride said, "we appear to be driving out of the city."

"Correct."

"I take it we aren't going to the city police building, then?"

Bolan realized they had walked into a setup and reached inside his jacket for the holstered Beretta.

Something hard was thrust ungraciously into his ribs.

"Not in the car, Mr. Belasko," Van Hooten advised softly. "It would make such a mess. And I'm supposed to deliver you unharmed. My little deception has worked so well up to now. Let us not spoil things."

The man beside the driver of the Volvo turned to face the rear seat, holding a large autopistol in his right hand. His lean features broke into a cold smile as he leveled the muzzle at Bolan's head.

"Take out your weapons," he said in heavily accented English, "very carefully. Then hand them to me."

Bolan did as he was told.

"I must also ask you to pass over the information the late Mr. Diel gave you," the inspector said. "And please do not insult me by saying you do not have it with you."

When the warrior handed over the envelope, Van Hooten tore it open and studied the contents.

"An extremely detailed package. I can appreciate why Diel wanted this in the hands of his superiors so urgently, and why you have been protecting it so strongly.'' Van Hooten leaned back against the padded rear of the seat. ''The next question is obvious.''

''You'll have to spell it out for me,'' Bolan said. ''I'm a little slow at the moment.''

''Play all the games you wish, my friend. Stall as much as you want. But in the end you will give us every last detail we wish to hear. My principals are going to need to know how much of Diel's information you have transmitted to your superiors. How much and to whom. It is important that they know as soon as possible.''

Bolan didn't reply, because there was nothing to tell. He hadn't had the opportunity to pass anything along. He had received Diel's information, digested it, and it had gone no further. Van Hooten's people didn't know that, nor would they believe him if he told them as much. They would do their worst to pry the information from him. The only thing the warrior could do was to try to string them along until an opportunity arose for him to go on the offensive.

The man leaning across the front seat lashed out with the barrel of his autopistol and rapped it across the side of Bolan's face. Blood began to stream down the side of the Executioner's face.

''The man asked you a question, Belasko. Be polite and answer him.''

''I have nothing to tell you.''

Van Hooten shrugged. ''I can accept that for now. But do not expect such lenient treatment at the hands of my principals. They are not very pleasant people.''

"José Contreros," Bolan said, "and the Colombian drug cartel."

"Correct," Van Hooten acknowledged.

"You work for them?" McBride asked.

"Of course, my dear young woman. They might be bad people in your eyes, but to me they are extremely competent businessmen. The money I receive from them is not soiled in any way. It is simply money. In large amounts, I might add, which only increases my loyalty toward them. Life, you see, is very uncomplicated."

"Doesn't it concern you that—"

"That I am a policeman sworn to uphold the law?" Van Hooten laughed out loud. "Please, do not embarrass me with your naïveté. We are living in a decadent world where the strong survive and a man's loyalty remains only until the paychecks stop coming. Don't waste your words on me. I have no bad dreams, and I sleep soundly."

Bolan sat back in the padded seat, digesting what Van Hooten had just told him. Things were clicking into place now. He didn't need to ask who had informed the Rotterdam traffickers he and Kelly McBride were in the city, or who had put them on to Evan Brewer. The Colombian drug dealer had been manipulating events quietly and calmly, issuing orders and letting Bolan eliminate the local opposition for him. And the warrior had done exactly that.

Although he hadn't met the Colombian, Bolan had to give him his due. Contreros showed flair.

TWENTY MINUTES LATER the Volvo and the car following pulled into the driveway of a large house. The city lay behind them now, flat landscape stretching in all directions. Tall trees stood in straight lines, following the placid ribbons of calm canals. Passing through open gates, the cars rolled along the graveled drive until they finally reached the redbrick facade of the three-story house. A number of cars stood in the parking area that fronted the building.

Daylight was slanting across the cold sky as Bolan was hauled from the Volvo. A rough hand at his back propelled him in the direction of the house. The main door opened, and armed figures flanked the entrance.

"Get them inside," Van Hooten snapped, all traces of his former geniality erased.

The Executioner walked through the door and found himself in a wide entrance hall. A curving staircase led to the upper floors. A door on his right opened and two men appeared.

"Took your bloody time," one of them said sharply.

"We cannot always follow the clock, Mr. Dekker," Van Hooten answered.

"I'll remember to tell Mr. Redland you said so." Dekker snapped his fingers at the armed men. "Get this pair in the library. We can't waste any more time."

Bolan turned slightly, catching Van Hooten's eye. The crooked cop felt a chill course down his spine. There was something in his prisoner's icy stare that made him distinctly uncomfortable.

"Make the most of your money, Van Hooten," Bolan said quietly. "Your time's almost up."

Van Hooten started a grin of defiance, but there was such an air of menace in the words that it fell short. He backed away.

"Are you going to kiss him goodbye, Van Hooten, or what? Just get the hell back to town and sort out the mess he left behind. It's what you're paid to do."

Bolan and McBride were hustled through the door into the library. They were seated in leather armchairs, with guards on either side of them.

The Executioner noticed the motionless figure seated behind the large desk at the far side of the room. The light was behind him, shadowing the man, but Bolan sensed he was looking at José Contreros. The figure rose and came round the desk to stand in front of Bolan.

He was of average height, with dark skin and black hair that was brushed straight back. His gaze settled on Bolan, a pleased smile edging his thin, taut mouth.

"I congratulate you, Mr. Belasko. You have not disappointed me. Annoyed me, perhaps, because your visit to Star Freight has caused us a great deal of inconvenience. Are you aware how many of our people you put out of action?"

Bolan didn't answer. He was recalling the voice he had heard on the mobile phone back in Amsterdam, the same voice he was listening to now.

"When I realized Mr. Redland's attempt to have you captured on the road had failed, I decided to make use of your talents in another way. Van Hooten was able to monitor your progress via his people in the police force. We almost lost you when you ditched your car in Leiden. By the time you reached Rotterdam we had you spotted again. Then we used local help."

"By feeding the Rotterdam traffickers information on where we were staying? And betraying one of your own contacts to them?"

Contreros laughed gently. "Yes to the first part. As to betraying Brewer, he had already shown he was not to be trusted. He had sold out his former colleagues by coming to me with the drug deal. Would you trust such a man once he had outlived his usefulness? I think not. He was a dead man anyway. Mr. Redland was not pleased about the background information concerning the weapons Brewer sold him."

"Your visit to the boat yard took out the top management of the Rotterdam syndicate," Dekker said. "Cleared the way for our takeover nicely."

"'Our takeover'?" Bolan queried.

"Let me explain," Contreros said. "Since my dealings with Mr. Redland and the way he handled the drug sale, I have realized he has the contacts and the capability of managing a continuing association with my organization. He has already made approaches to Mr. Mdofa. We will be discussing the fine details very shortly."

"Hell of a big continent, Africa," Dekker said.

"You miserable bastards," McBride yelled. "Isn't there enough suffering there already? Now you want to flood the country with drugs."

"Market forces, my dear. You go where there's a need." Contreros ran a manicured hand over his hair. "It is no different than a McDonald's in Moscow."

Dekker glanced at his watch, then spoke quietly to Contreros, who nodded.

Turning, Dekker gestured to a slim figure seated at the side of the room. The man straightened and approached Bolan and McBride.

"You will each roll up a sleeve," he ordered.

"What are you doing?" McBride asked, alarmed.

"Just something to relax you," the man replied, holding up a pair of filled hypodermic syringes. "Nothing to worry about."

Dekker grinned. "The worry comes when you wake up."

In the background Contreros was chuckling as he picked up a telephone and began to talk.

The injections were over quickly.

"Don't fight it," the man said. "You can't resist for long, so just let yourselves go."

He was right. Bolan began to feel the room rock a little. The motion increased. Objects began to slip in and out of focus. A sensation of deep warmth flooded his very being, pushing away all thoughts of discomfort and pain. Worry evaporated. Soft colors filled his mind. Sound was distant, then close, calming. He did try to resist the sensations, but already his body was weak. It became too much for him to fight, so he gave up trying and slipped into the rich, enveloping darkness. . . .

13

Bolan drifted in and out of a deep, heavy sleep. He couldn't count how many times he slid from darkness into a misty grayness where nothing gelled. He was aware of mixed sensations. Of floating. Being surrounded by a soft, droning whisper of sound. When he tried to move he found his limbs slow to respond. The effort proved too strenuous, and the darkness reached out to claim him again. When he awakened again, his eyes focused on a sallow, unresponsive face that looked distorted. He saw the mouth moving, but the only sound he heard was too far away and garbled. He tried to sit up, but hands pressed him down. A thin hand appeared in his field of vision, holding a needle. A sharp pain pricked his arm, and everything turned to fuzz again. He slid away from reality, back down the black tunnel to his endless sleep....

His final return to awareness came gradually, over a long time. His senses returned at will. Sound. Sight. Smell. Rising and falling, but coming back stronger each time. Bolan, aware of his weakness, made no attempt to move until he was certain he could actually manage to control his own actions.

He lay looking up at a whitewashed ceiling, hairline cracks in the coat of paint marring the surface. There were cobwebs in the corner he could see. Movement caught Bolan's attention, and he eased his aching head around gently, eyes seeking the source.

A speckled lizard crawled sedately across the ceiling, its long dark tongue flicking out.

Bolan became conscious of the heat now. It was intense, heavy and oppressive, and it bore down on him like a thick blanket. Even the air was hot.

When he moved restlessly on the cot on which he lay, he felt it sway under him, creaking against loose, dry joints.

He lifted a hand and touched his face. Thick stubble rasped against his fingers. The flesh beneath was moist with sweat.

The Executioner sat up slowly, eased his legs over the side of the cot and dropped them to the floor—a hard-packed dirt floor.

Nausea welled up from his stomach. He gripped the edge of the cot and sat still until the sickness passed. He realized how weak he still was. He needed time for his body to pull itself together. He began to breathe, deeply and slowly, closing his mind to everything around him.

Time passed unnoticed.

Somewhere in the near distance Bolan could hear voices and the low rumble of machinery.

He pushed up off the cot and stood, swaying until his body settled. He was about to take his first step when the door to the room crashed open.

The mercenary called Dekker stood there, watching Bolan, a half grin on his face.

"You thinking of leaving us?"

Dekker came into the room, followed by two men carrying Uzis. They stood on either side of Bolan.

"If you're feeling so bloody energetic, Belasko, we might as well leave right now. There's a truck waiting for you outside, ready to take you for a ride. Somebody wants to see you very badly."

Bolan felt hands grip his arms, then the pair of gunners propelled him from the room.

The unrelenting heat struck him the moment they stepped outside. Bright light hurt his eyes, sound attacked him from all sides and smells assailed his nostrils.

Color and noise dazzled him.

Yellow dust puffed up from beneath his feet as he was hustled across dry, parched earth. A skeletal dog, its eyes plagued by flies, limped across their path.

Bolan stared about him, adjusting to the noise and the heat and the glare. He knew where he was without having to be told. This wasn't Holland, this was Chandra.

On the continent of Africa.

THE TRUCK STOPPED with a jerk, throwing Bolan off the bench seat. He crashed to the floor, unable to stop himself because of his bound hands. The side of his head rapped against the boards, and he felt pain flare through one shoulder.

"Get him on his damn feet," Dekker snapped at the other two mercs.

FIND OUT INSTANTLY THE GIFTS YOU GET ABSOLUTELY FREE!

LUCKY CARNIVAL WHEEL

▼ SCRATCH-OFF GAME! ▼

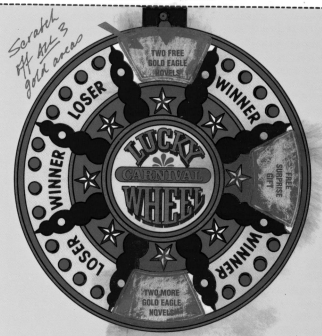

Scratch Off ALL 3 gold areas

YES! I have scratched off the 3 Gold Areas above. Please send me all the gifts to which I am entitled. I understand I am under no obligation to purchase any books, as explained on the back and on the opposite page.   164 CIM AQ3T
(U-M-B-01/95)

NAME

ADDRESS   APT.

CITY   STATE   ZIP

Hands locked on to Bolan's arms, and he was hauled upright. He was marched to the tailgate of the truck and manhandled to the ground.

"Inside," Dekker ordered.

Bolan was pushed in the direction of a low building. He was given little opportunity to check his surroundings. All he managed was a quick glimpse of a dusty, sunbaked area crowded with armed, uniformed men. In the distance he spotted a wire fence and guard towers. It was a military compound of some kind.

He was shoved through a door. The room inside was bleak, functional, dim after the exterior brightness. Voices in the distance had a military ring to them. He was pushed against a wall and told to stand still.

Dekker and his two comrades stood a few yards away. They appeared relaxed, comfortable in familiar surroundings. When Bolan locked eyes with Dekker, the merc had a thin smile on his lips.

"Ready to rock and roll, hotshot?" the merc asked. "We'll see how tough you really are soon, see if you squeal before you die. Diel went the hard way when we cornered him. He was a tough bastard, but even the hard ones die in the end."

Bolan looked away as a group of men, most of them in military uniform, entered the room from the rear of the building. The majority of them were armed, and he recognized the one in the lead immediately. He had seen the face before in the news media.

Tall and lean, the cheeks of his gaunt face marked by tribal scars, Lenard Mdofa walked erect, eyes bright with the fanatic's stare. He was immaculate in army fatigues, his combat boots gleaming. On his right hip he wore a holstered SIG-Sauer P-226 auto-pistol.

"This is the one?" he asked. His voice was crisp, reeking of an expensive and private British education, the words delivered with taut precision.

Dekker nodded. "Calls himself Belasko."

Mdofa glanced at Bolan as if he were something scraped off the sole of a boot.

"How many did he kill?"

"Enough," Dekker acknowledged.

"Mr. Redland should have been recruiting a man like this—not having him hunted down because he works for the opposition." Mdofa turned to Dekker. "The woman?"

"Brought in by a different route from the airstrip."

"Good." Mdofa nodded. "Lock them in separate cells. Allow them to rest for a few hours, and then we will talk. Tonight. When it is cooler."

Bolan was pushed past Mdofa and his retinue. Almost as an afterthought the tall African caught hold of Bolan's shirt and spun him to face him.

"By the way, Mr. Belasko, allow me to welcome you to our beautiful country. Unfortunately your stay will be brief. Educational but brief...."

BOLAN USED HIS TIME alone wisely, resting as much as he could. His body was still weak from the drug-enforced sleep, and he knew it could be some time before he gained his full strength again.

His cell, constructed from concrete blocks, with one barred wall open to the fenced-off compound, gave him the opportunity to study much of the area. From where he sat on the low cot bolted to the floor, Bolan was able to see directly across the dusty compound to the main gate. It was flanked on both sides by high sentry towers. Each tower was occupied by a two-man team equipped with a machine gun that was mounted centrally, so that it could be swiveled to cover both inside and outside the compound.

To the far right of Bolan's cell was the motor pool, where there was an assortment of vehicles, ranging from 4x4 all-terrain vehicles to large troop-carrying trucks. In the middle of the compound was a concrete helicopter pad, large enough to handle at least three aircraft. Two choppers were parked there now. One was a Hind gunship, the other a smaller craft capable of carrying a pilot and passenger. Bolan's keen eyes picked out a fuel dump, with hundreds of drums stacked in neat rows. The landing pad and the fuel dump were constantly patrolled by armed Africans clad in desert camou fatigues.

More men moved around the compound in a seemingly endless stream. It appeared that Lenard Mdofa had himself quite an army.

Bolan was also quick to note the presence of at least a dozen white men. They were dressed in a mixture of outfits, but they were all armed, and they all moved with the casual ease of professional military personnel—Liam Redland's mercenaries, the hired soldiers working for Mdofa.

BOLAN HEARD the 4x4 as it rolled up to his cell. It stopped yards away and a tall, lean-faced man in tan

pants and shirt climbed out. Around his waist was a
web belt, and high-ride holster that showed the butt of
an autopistol. He stopped in front of Bolan's cell,
easing off the sunglasses he was wearing, so he could
get a clear picture of the tall, dark-haired man inside
the cell.

"I'm going to enjoy making you talk, Belasko,"
Liam Redland said. "You've cost me a great deal. If
we lose that weapons container on top of everything
else, I promise to make what's left of your life extremely unpleasant."

Bolan refrained from making any reply. There
wasn't anything to be gained from engaging in a ma-
cho show of words with Redland. The merc was no
fool. He was testing his prisoner, trying to find a chink
in his armor. Bolan's refusal to rise to Redland's bait-
ing told the merc he was dealing with a professional.
It wasn't about to make the Executioner's life any
easier, but it *did* mean that Redland would treat Bolan with caution.

A man in the passenger seat of the 4x4 leaned out of
the shade and raised a mocking hand in Bolan's direction. It was José Contreros. Dressed in cool, light-
weight clothing, he appeared relaxed and confident in
his new surroundings.

Redland turned abruptly, returned to his vehicle and
left the compound.

A flurry of movement caught Bolan's attention. He
watched a truck backing up to a loading platform at
the front of a low, windowless building. The canvas
flap at the rear of the truck was lifted, and boxes were
passed from the vehicle and onto the loading plat-

form. Bolan recognized the boxes as military packaging. More weaponry for Mdofa's arsenal. The building he was looking at was precisely that—the storage facility for the arms Mdofa was gathering.

The warrior spent some time familiarizing himself with the building. He watched as the unloading was completed and the truck pulled away. The crowd of helpers dispersed, leaving only the six armed guards to resume their patrolling of the building.

The door to Bolan's cell rattled and swung open. An armed guard appeared, gesturing for the Executioner to remain where he was. A second man stepped into the cell, carrying a wooden tray that held a clay pot of water. A second bowl contained a watery stew. The guard placed the tray on the floor and backed out of the cell. The armed escort followed him, and the door was slammed shut and locked.

Bolan crossed to the tray, picked it up and took it back to the cot. He ate the meager meal, then pressed his back to the wall and considered his options. The prospects were thin.

He was here so that Redland and Mdofa could try to dig out whatever they thought Bolan could tell them. Their main concern would be the extent of his knowledge of their organization and what he had done with it.

The success of the intended coup against Victor Joffi depended on keeping the operation secret. The possibility of the Executioner having passed any of the information received from Diel would be uppermost in the minds of the conspirators. If the U.S. authorities gained the knowledge of a planned coup against a recognized and democratically elected figure such as Joffi, there would have been frantic diplomatic moves to inform the Chandran administration. Mdofa's advantage would have been lost, his carefully orchestrated plans wasted and his future chances reduced considerably.

The immediate future didn't hold much comfort as far as Bolan was concerned. His life expectancy could be shortened considerably as long as he remained a captive. His only chances lay in escaping as soon as possible.

Mdofa was intent on surviving, which was why he had Bolan under his control.

And Mack Bolan had no intention of rolling over and giving up simply to allow the rebel to have his way. So in the end it came down to a simple choice: staying alive, or dying.

Charlie Diel hadn't been allowed the privilege. His life had been taken from him by violent men intent on concealing their illegal dealings. Kelly McBride had been plunged headlong into the relentless helter-skelter of death and betrayal simply because she had tried to help a friend. Jan Wender had been casually murdered simply by being in the wrong place at the wrong time.

The list was growing with every passing minute. It was time to have the slate wiped clean.

Payback time.

14

The room was bare except for two hard wooden chairs bolted to the concrete floor, with leather straps attached to the arms and legs. There was also one fixed to the backrest, intended to restrain head movement. The room was devoid of windows. Illumination was provided by a powerful lamp set in the ceiling. It threw a hard, cold wash of stark light into every corner of the room. The walls were covered by a coating of thin plaster, stained with rusty streaks and splashes. Similar marks were on the floor, especially around the bolted-down chairs.

Dekker was already in the room, with two of his armed mercs, when Bolan was brought in.

"In the chair," Dekker snapped.

The armed Africans who had collected Bolan from his cell pushed him to one of the chairs. At a gesture from Dekker they left the room, pulling the heavy door shut behind them.

The merc moved around so he was facing Bolan. "From here on in it's down to you, Belasko. Personally I don't give a damn if you end up in little chunks. If you want pain, you can have it. One way or the other we'll get what we want. So why don't you make it easy on yourself? Why end up with a lot of grief over this? You don't owe this country a thing. Why take the flak?''

''Maybe I don't like what you boys are planning.''

Dekker shook his head. ''All of a sudden we get bleeding hearts coming out of the woodwork. What is it with you?''

Bolan caught Dekker's stare and held it for several long seconds.

Then Dekker moved, his right fist sweeping around to slam against Bolan's left cheek. The blow shoved the warrior off the chair and onto the concrete floor, the impact driving the air from his lungs. He lay where he'd fallen, tasting blood in his mouth from a tooth-cut cheek.

''Pick him up,'' Dekker said wearily, realizing he had a stubborn one on his hands. He waited until Bolan had been deposited back on the chair, then the merc leaned in close. ''Understand this, Belasko, and believe. You are very close to being dead. So close I can smell it.''

Bolan lifted his head. A large bruise was already forming on his cheek.

''Killing me isn't going to get you any answers.''

''A smartass, as well,'' Dekker said. ''I bloody hate smartasses—especially when they're the Yank version.''

Dekker's temper got the better of him, and he began to hit Bolan hard, but not hard enough to do irreparable damage. The blows to the warrior's face and body were intended to hurt, not maim.

''Hey, don't kill him, Dek,'' one of the mercs called out. ''Mdofa doesn't like his game dead before he has his chance. And Liam isn't going to be too happy about you jumping the gun.''

"That pair is too busy making their deals with the drug king,'' Dekker snapped back, showing his feeling for Mdofa and Redland. ''It'll make them sit up when we get this Yank to spill his guts.''

He finally stopped the beating and stepped back from Bolan's bloody form.

"Belasko, don't be a damn fool,'' he said. ''All we need are a few answers.''

The Executioner raised his battered face and stared at the merc.

"I've got nothing to say.''

"Son of a bitch,'' Dekker said and turned away. ''Go get the woman. We'll try the soft route.''

Mack Bolan concentrated on the deep well of his reserves, the part of him that had no physical substance but which sustained him, as it had before, during times of hardship. It kept him aware of his immediate condition, able to override pain and allow him to perform despite his injuries.

He had registered Dekker's order to bring in Kelly. His refusal to capitulate to the merc's physical attack had pushed the man toward an alternative tack.

Kelly's presence in the room would offer Bolan a slight advantage.

When he made his move, which was going to have to be sooner rather than later, he wouldn't have to go searching for the young woman. The other, more basic, gain was Kelly's physical presence. The opportunity to abuse an attractive female captive wouldn't be lost on Dekker and his merc partners. Bolan would have to make the best of that chance because it was going to be his only one.

THE DOOR OPENED and Kelly McBride was pushed into the room. Behind her the grinning merc closed the door and slammed home the bolt.

"No getting out, honey," he drawled.

And no one getting in, Bolan thought.

McBride looked tired and shaky. Her clothing was stained and creased, her thick hair tangled.

"Say hello to a friend," Dekker said, stepping aside so that Bolan was exposed.

The woman let out an audible gasp when she saw Bolan's battered, bloody face.

"Mike!"

Bolan feigned deafness, keeping his gaze fixed on the wall behind McBride.

"He's feeling a little delicate right now," Dekker explained. "We've been having a discussion about needs and wants. I need answers to questions. He doesn't want to give them. It leaves us with something of an impasse."

"So we thought you might be able to break it," one of the mercs said. "Right, Dek?"

Dekker nodded. "Couldn't have put it better myself, Tucker."

Tucker moved to lean his autofire against the wall, then turned and grabbed McBride's wrist. He swung her up against the closest wall with a thump that made her gasp in pain. Before she could protect herself, Tucker slapped her hard across the face. McBride tried to hit out with her free hand, but Tucker slapped it aside, then punched her in the stomach. The woman sagged against the wall. Over his shoulder Tucker called to the other merc.

"Help me keep her on her feet, Rick."

The second merc joined him, transferring his rifle to his left hand as he caught hold of McBride's other arm.

"Dek?"

Dekker reached to the rear of his belt and slid out a keen-bladed knife from a sheath. He tapped the side of Bolan's face.

"Wake up, Belasko, this is for your benefit. Decision time. The lady gets cut up if you don't start giving the right sort of answers. If you don't care about her, we'll soon know."

Across the room Tucker snatched at the front of McBride's shirt, tearing buttons free as he yanked it open. For the next few seconds he and Rick were absorbed in staring at the woman's exposed flesh.

"Last call, Belasko," Dekker said lightly, turning away from the immobile figure, the blade of his knife catching light as he moved.

Bolan was watching the knife as Dekker turned. He waited for his chance, then rose from the chair in a fluid movement. His left hand snapped around the merc's neck, pulling the man off balance, while his right caught Dekker's knife wrist. The warrior twisted, turning the blade in toward Dekker's own body. Then he shoved hard, pushing the knife into the merc's body. The sleek blade entered easily, slicing through flesh to penetrate deep into the torso. Dekker arched in agony, then gasped as Bolan used his momentum to drag the blade across the man's body, twisting it at the same time.

Tucker and Rick, sensing the flurry of movement beyond their main vision, began to respond.

Bolan removed the knife from Dekker's twitching fingers and shoved the dying man aside as he dropped to a crouch, lunging forward. The bloody knife was held before him in an equally bloody hand. The warrior reached Rick as the merc tried to bring his rifle into play.

The knife flashed up and around. Rick felt a pin-prick of pain across his throat, thinking nothing of it until moments later when the knife slash to his throat developed into a bloody fountain. He stumbled back against the wall, dropping his rifle and clutching at his throat. Hot blood began to course over his fingers, and the merc lost all interest in the proceedings as he fought a losing battle against staying alive.

Tucker had spun away from McBride, making for the rifle he had leaned against the wall. He knew he wasn't going to reach it, so he went for the gun holstered on his hip. He closed his fingers over the butt and began to draw it free.

Bolan slammed into his side. The impact shoved Tucker into the wall, trapping his gun hand. He panicked, remembering the bloody knife in his adversary's hand.

Rolling across the wall, Tucker faced the man he knew as Belasko. The red-bladed knife swept in fast, and Tucker threw up an arm to block it. Bolan pulled back, so that the edge of the knife slashed across the merc's exposed arm, cutting in deep.

Tucker felt blood pulsing thickly over his arm and when he looked, he was shocked to see the extent of the damage. The merc pushed away, still trying for his handgun. Bolan thrust out and up with the knife. The tip slid in under Tucker's jaw, slicing into the soft flesh. Bolan put all of his weight behind the thrust, sinking the blade up to the hilt.

The merc snatched at the handle of the knife, already slick with blood, but it had wedged against his jawbone and refused to move. He slumped at the base of the wall, moaning softly, his body shuddering against the onset of pain from the intruding steel lodged in his throat.

Bolan freed the handgun from Tucker's holster. It was a heavy Desert Eagle, the same model as the one taken from him back in Rotterdam. He checked the clip then replaced it, making certain the safety was on before he jammed it under his belt. Reaching for the AK-74 autorifle leaning against the wall, Bolan turned to where McBride crouched.

"It's time we got out of here," he said gently.

McBride looked up at him. For the first time since he'd met her, Bolan saw tears in her eyes. He helped her to her feet.

"I would have stopped it sooner," he said, "but they needed to be distracted first."

McBride managed a smile. "Glad I was some use." She examined his face. "Mike, what have they done to you?"

"I'll survive."

Bolan picked up the second rifle, another AK-74, and removed the 30-round 5.45 mm magazine. He slipped it into a pocket of his blacksuit and zipped it up. Bending over Dekker's motionless figure, he eased out the dead merc's handgun, a 9 mm Browning Hi-Power.

"Can you handle one of these?" he asked Mc-Bride.

She took the weapon. "I've checked out on most handguns," she admitted. "It comes with being a military brat."

"Your father?"

"Yes. He was a Marine."

"Maybe we've got a chance then," Bolan said and moved for the door.

"Mike, this is crazy. Do you expect all those men out there to stand back while we walk away?"

Bolan slid the bolt free and began to ease open the door.

"Nobody said it was going to be easy."

McBride moved up behind Bolan as he peered through the crack in the door.

Beyond the door the hallway stretched the length of the building, with cell doors on either side. At the far end was a door fitted with a barred grille. Bolan could see open sky through the grille.

"We head straight for the door at the far end. You watch our backs. If anybody shows, don't ask for ID. Just shoot. We'll get one chance in here. After that it won't matter."

The woman shook her head. "You sure know how to give a girl a good time, Belasko."

Bolan flipped off the autorifle's safety as he moved into the passage.

"I'm just getting started," he replied tightly.

15

There was no one standing guard on the other side of the door. Bolan and McBride had been the only prisoners in the cell block, and with Dekker and his armed mercs present, security wouldn't have appeared a problem—until Dekker had decided to begin the interrogation early.

Pressed tight against the door, Bolan glanced down at his wristwatch, then realized there was no point in expecting his timepiece to guide him. They were in a different time zone.

"I'd say it'll be dark within fifteen to twenty minutes," McBride informed him. "The sun's already going down."

Bolan nodded. He was checking out the area on the other side of the door. Across from them was the rear of what looked like a mess hall, with a kitchen attached. Cooking stoves threw smoke into the air from tin chimneys jutting out through the wooden roof. The warrior studied the building closely. His mind was working swiftly, attempting to come up with an effective, but off-the-cuff plan of action.

There was little chance he and Kelly could make their break during daylight hours. And despite Kelly telling him they only had half an hour to wait before dark, Bolan knew they were stretching the odds. So they needed some kind of distraction, something that could draw the attention of the occupants of the compound long enough for night to fall. With darkness their chances improved greatly. Still no guarantees, but at least a fighting chance.

"I have to get over there," Bolan said, "to the kitchen."

"Why?"

"We need to divert attention away from us for a while. At least until it gets dark."

"Explain."

"I set a fire. Get that place blazing. It should keep them busy. Give us a chance to hide away somewhere until we can chance a break out of here."

He studied the building again. It was raised off the ground, leaving a crawl space underneath that was littered with boxes and cans. The open ground between the cell block and the kitchen was flat and exposed, but it was also deserted. The rear of the mess hall was an area left to the cooks and their helpers.

"The longer we wait, the less time we're going to have," the warrior added.

He eased open the door and checked the immediate area. The closest activity was off to their left. A group of uniformed men clustered around an instructor who was showing them how to strip down and reassemble a light machine gun. They were at least a hundred yards away.

"We go straight across," Bolan said. "Don't hesitate. Keep low, but move under the kitchen area to the side of those boxes. Stay down and stay still."

McBride nodded and followed Bolan out the door. They paused long enough to make certain no one was looking their way. Then the warrior tapped her on the shoulder and she took off for the distant building. It looked much farther away now. But she took his advice and simply headed straight for it, clutching the handgun as if it were the most important thing in her life.

Behind her, Bolan made the run with single-minded determination. He tried to keep noise down to the minimum, but to his ears the sound of their passing seemed overly loud. He tried to ignore the feeling, though he expected a bullet in the back.

Nothing happened.

They threw themselves flat under the floorboards of the kitchen, trying not to cough as dust rose to irritate their nostrils. Bolan pushed against McBride's taut buttocks, guiding her unceremoniously. She wriggled in behind cover, the Executioner sliding alongside, and they lay for a while panting heavily. Sweat beaded their faces and stung their eyes. Bolan's bruised and bloody face only added to his discomfort.

He handed McBride the AK-74. She took it and watched as her companion wriggled to where a number of five-gallon cans were lined up in the shade of the crawl space. Peering at the drums, she saw they contained cooking oil. Bolan rolled a couple out from under the building, righted them and unscrewed the caps.

As he crouched close to cane baskets holding piles of vegetables, the warrior looked up the wooden steps that led to the kitchen. He raised himself so he could see inside. The range of cooking stoves, primitive boxes constructed from sheet metal, radiated heat from the burning wood inside. On the far side of the kitchen were cooking benches that held an assortment of pots, pans, bowls and utensils. A single African, sweating in soiled whites, toiled over food preparation. He carried a holstered handgun on his hip. Beyond the kitchen area, Bolan was able to make out rows of mess tables and benches. Men were moving up and down between the tables, preparing them for the evening meal.

The Executioner took one of the oil drums and lifted it to the top of the steps. He repeated the operation with the second drum.

The expectation of discovery was a strong motivator, driving Bolan forward, making him push aside caution as he mounted the steps, keeping his eyes on the armed cook.

The warrior reached down for the first drum, spreading his feet and bracing himself. One of the dry boards underfoot creaked loudly.

The cook turned, his eyes wide with surprise as he saw Bolan in the act of lifting the drum of oil. He muttered to himself and went for the gun on his hip, fumbling with the retaining strap.

Bolan didn't hesitate. He hoisted the drum, oil spurting from the opening, and threw it bodily at the man. The drum hit the guy in the center of the chest, knocking him back across his table, scattering its contents.

The Executioner turned and grabbed the second drum, tipped it and allowed oil to gush out over the floorboards. The golden liquid spread and soaked into the dry wood. He dumped the drum on the floor where it continued to empty itself as it rolled.

The dazed cook, pushing aside the offending drum, rolled to his feet, still groping for his handgun. His upper body and hands glistened with oil. When he managed to free the autopistol, it slipped from his oily fingers and bounced across the floor. Cursing, the cook snatched a knife from the table. He turned, searching for the intruder, and spotted Bolan just as he put one foot against the rear of a cook stove and upended it. The stove toppled with a crash, the chimney breaking free with a clatter. Soot and smoke billowed out across the kitchen. Blazing embers of wood spewed out of the stove, scattering across the floor. The spilled oil ignited, and flames spread swiftly. They raced across the liquid, being fed by the stream of oil still gushing from the drum.

Bolan stood for a few seconds watching the racing flames. The pace was almost too fast for him. He turned and cleared the steps seconds before the kitchen area was engulfed, fire reaching out and up, rolling as high as the rafters of the roof apex. The tinder-dry wood caught rapidly.

The warrior scrambled under the building to where McBride lay. Smoke was already creeping through the floorboards, and they could feel the heat of the fire. Taking back the rifle, Bolan pointed the way. He and his companion crawled to the far side of the building, away from the kitchen. The far side butted onto an area where building materials had been stacked. They cleared the building and moved in among the long stacks of planks and poles.

Behind them the mess hall was being rapidly swallowed by the fire. Smoke billowed into the lowering sky, blotting out the setting sun. Above the crackle and roar of the flames they could hear shouts as the alarm was raised.

Bolan checked out the area and spotted parked vehicles behind them. Touching McBride's arm, Bolan indicated the vehicles. They crawled in that direction, pausing to check for guards. None. The Executioner led the way in among the vehicles. He picked out a fuel tanker. They slid under the chassis and bellied down in the weed-choked shadows.

"Mike, they'll start to look for us soon," McBride said. "It won't take long for them to find out we're loose."

Bolan didn't answer at once. He was checking out the area and trying to keep an eye on the men closing on the blazing building. He needed to keep himself and his companion free and clear until darkness fell. The night would bring them natural cover, and they could use that to their advantage.

There were no guarantees. The onset of darkness didn't mean they wouldn't be spotted, or make their escape unharmed. Life just didn't work that way. The odds had a habit of changing, and there was no way of altering the law of circumstance. It was purely a matter of going with the flow.

"Mike?"

Bolan glanced at her. "We keep moving," he replied, "and look out for a vehicle we can use."

"Hertz okay?" she suggested dryly. "Hope you've got cash, 'cause I lost my card somewhere along the way."

Bolan picked up the nervous tremor in her voice. The light banter was Kelly's way of handling her fear.

The sound of a dull explosion caught their attention. Something had blown within the blazing kitchen, sending tendrils of flame arcing in all directions. Figures scattered, ducking and weaving to avoid being struck by the fiery spirals. Sparks soared skyward in the clouds of dense smoke.

Bolan used the explosion to move himself and McBride farther away. They eased in between the parked vehicles, ducking out of sight when armed figures showed briefly as they passed.

"Are they looking for us?" McBride asked, sensing the urgency in Bolan's movements.

He nodded, bringing the AK-74 into the firing position. Gesturing her to move behind him, Bolan scanned the area. The motor pool would offer them only temporary protection. Sooner or later Mdofa's men would flush them out.

They heard the rumble of an engine, then saw the squat shape of an open-backed Land Rover edging around the perimeter of the motor pool. Behind the driver a uniformed African hung on to the firing handles of a swivel-mounted Browning .50-caliber machine gun. The Land Rover was moving slowly, giving the gunner time to peer in among the parked vehicles.

"Stay close," Bolan said.

He began to track the Land Rover. When it reached the extreme edge of the motor pool it made a tight left turn, following the line of the parking area.

"We'll get one chance," Bolan said. "If we can grab that Rover, we head for the gates. Straight through and out."

He watched her reaction. There was fear of what might lie ahead, but that was good. He would have been concerned if she had accepted his decision without question.

"As soon as we hit the Rover you take the wheel. We go around the far side of the mess hall, then cut across to the right. Make a run past the helicopter pad, then straight out toward the gates."

Bolan was sketching a swift diagram in the dust as he spoke. He indicated the directions he wanted Kelly to follow.

"Whatever happens, just keep going. Pedal to the floor and go."

She stared at him, wide-eyed with nervousness.

"We could die doing this, couldn't we, Mike?"

The warrior looked her straight in the eye. "We could. But we're not going to. We'll hit them so fast they won't know how to fight us off."

He made a quick check of the AK-74. McBride eased off the Hi-Power's safety and snapped the slide back to cock the handgun. She held it in a two-handed combat grip, her actions backing up her claim to familiarity with weapons.

Bolan moved through the close-parked vehicles, getting ahead of the slow-moving Land Rover. He pressed hard against the rear of a truck, crouching to peer beneath the chassis. He could see the wheels of the Land Rover moving his way. Checking out the immediate vicinity, he saw no other movement.

"Move out," he snapped at McBride.

Bolan eased himself around the end of the truck, bringing the AK-74 to his shoulder. As the Land Rover crawled into view, the warrior rose partway and triggered a short burst that took the vehicle's driver in the head and upper chest. The man uttered a strangled cry and pitched out of his seat, sprawling in the dust on the far side of the Land Rover. The vehicle lurched a couple of yards before it jerked to a stop and the engine stalled.

In the back of the vehicle the gunner broke into action, hauling the Browning around on its swivel and angling the barrel over the side.

Bolan's AK-74 was already tracking him. The Executioner triggered a swift burst that pulped the guy's left shoulder. As his arm dropped, useless and bloody at his side, the gunner continued to swivel the machine gun.

There was a flicker of movement at Bolan's side. McBride stepped out from cover, the Hi-Power picking up on the gunner. She triggered a pair of shots with cool precision, the 9 mm slugs coring into the gunner's forehead. He toppled over and dropped to the ground.

The moment she'd fired, McBride sprinted for the stalled Land Rover. Sliding into the driver's seat, she buckled the seat belt and bent to start the vehicle. As the engine burst into life, Bolan vaulted into the rear.

He laid the AK-74 on the bed of the open body and grabbed the machine gun's trigger handles.

"Hang on," McBride yelled as she dropped the gears into reverse and brought around the Land Rover in a swirl of choking dust.

Bolan braced himself as the Land Rover picked up speed. McBride followed his directions to the letter. Sweeping around the edge of the motor pool, she cut across toward the blazing mess hall, into the drifting smoke and out the other side, scattering shouting men in her wake. More than once the Land Rover struck something yielding.

The sudden appearance of the racing vehicle caught Mdofa's men unprepared. Those around the mess hall were concentrating on the fire, and the hurtling Land Rover came and went before many of them realized. A few hasty shots followed in the vehicle's dusty wake.

They cleared the smoke, and McBride hauled on the wheel, taking the Land Rover in a slithering turn that put them on line for the helipad.

They became increasingly vulnerable now that they were in the open. Armed hardmen appeared and began to direct their fire at the Land Rover. Most shots fell short, but some clanged against the vehicle's sides.

Bolan primed the big Browning. He swiveled the weapon and let loose a short burst that sent .50-caliber shells at the closest group. The hammering roar of the big gun drowned out every other sound. The Executioner could feel the hot shell cases raining around his feet. A number of men went down, the rest scattered. Swinging the gun around, Bolan delivered a second, longer burst that drove more hardmen to cover.

Glancing over his shoulder, the warrior saw the helipad coming up fast. He leaned in over the back of the driver's seat and tapped McBride's shoulder.

"Skirt the choppers. It's the fuel dump I'm interested in."

She nodded.

Bolan had been checking out the equipment in the driver's compartment. Beside the seat was a weapons rack that held a pair of combat shotguns and a signal flare gun. He reached over and grabbed it, broke the breech and checked the load. Pulling himself back to the machine gun, he tucked the flare gun in his belt.

"Vehicle coming up on the left," McBride yelled. Her words were punctuated by the stammer of small-caliber autofire.

Bolan swiveled the Browning and looked down the barrel at a fast-moving 4x4 that was drawing level. The vehicle was painted with camou markings. Armed hardmen hung out of the open windows, trying to settle their aim, made difficult by the rough ride.

The Executioner had the advantage of a larger weapon that was mounted on a spring swivel designed to absorb the motion of the Land Rover. He sighted in on the 4x4's engine compartment and triggered a sustained burst. The high-impact .50-caliber shells ripped the thin body panels apart and fractured the engine block. As the 4x4 began to falter, Bolan tracked back and laid a second burst into the passenger compartment. The 4x4 swerved, tipped and rolled. It bounced and crashed its way across the compound, coming to final rest in a cloud of dust and oily smoke. Those inside who were still able to move had no time to crawl out before the wrecked vehicle burst into flame.

Bolan turned the Browning as McBride brought them alongside the neatly stacked fuel drums. At his command she eased off the pedal, letting the Land Rover coast. The warrior opened fire, stitching the rows of steel drums from top to bottom. As the ragged holes began to spew out gallons of liquid, Bolan pulled the flare gun from his belt and eased back the hammer. He aimed at the glistening pool of fuel and sent the signal flare directly into the center. The gasoline ignited with terrifying swiftness, feeding itself on the continuing streams pumping out of punctured drums. The blast of flame reached out in every direction, and Bolan saw that it was liable to catch up with the Land Rover.

"Kelly, hit that pedal!" he yelled, turning his back on the wash of heat.

The Land Rover sped across the compound, heading for the gates. Bolan, hunched over the Browning, felt the searing fingers of heat reach out and penetrate his clothing. He raised his head and peered over the Land Rover's windshield. The closed wooden gates of the compound lay ahead.

Armed hardmen were converging on the area, and the machine gunners in the towers were turning their weapons toward the compound.

"Mike!" McBride yelled in warning.

"Go for the gates!" he shouted back, because there was nothing else they could do now. They were fully committed to their actions.

He brought the machine gun into play, swiveling it right and left, laying down a murderous hail of .50-caliber death that scattered the advancing figures.

Shells tore up the ground just short of the speeding Land Rover as one of the tower gunners opened up, the shootist trying to get his range. It was difficult for the tower gunners. The approaching Land Rover was a high-speed target, calling for instant range adjustment with each passing second, and the gunners were having problems keeping up with it.

The Executioner leaned back, raising the Browning's barrel. His targets were static, giving him a slight advantage, and he took it. His first burst chewed at the wood supports of the tower. His second, aimed higher, blasted through the planking around the machine-gun nest. The two-man team was shredded by a deadly mix of .50-caliber shells and flying splinters of raw wood. Their world exploded in a red-hot scream of pain that mercifully ended in death.

The second tower let go a short burst before the weapon jammed. As the feed belt locked and the gun fell silent, the loader abandoned the weapon and picked up his autorifle. He leaned over the edge of the tower and opened fire with an AK-74. He saw most of his bullets fall short, but experienced a moment of satisfaction when he saw the driver of the Land Rover jerk sideways. The red-haired woman, whom he had seen arriving earlier that day, fought to regain control of the vehicle and succeeded.

Moments later the earth rocked and the tower swayed. The twilight sky lighted up as a huge ball of roaring flame, boiling like some primeval eruption of molten lava, filled the compound with its naked power.

The searching flames from the burning fuel had reached into the very heart of the dump, creating the conditions that precipitated the eruption of the entire stock. Thousands of gallons of stored fuel blew in a gigantic explosion. Flaming drums were hurled in all directions, causing more damage to buildings and men. Blazing fuel rained across the compound, engulfing everything it touched, scorching and shriveling anything that fell beneath its awful power. The shock wave from the blast turned vehicles on their sides and hurled men for yards.

In the seconds of the initial blast, Mack Bolan turned the full fury of the Browning machine gun on the compound gates. He held the triggers down and concentrated the devastating firepower of the .50-caliber weapon on the center section of the gates. The powerful shells ripped fist-size chunks of wood from the frames, weakening the structure and the drop bar that held the gates secure. When the Land Rover's crash bar impacted with the gates, the solid mass burst the gates open. The Land Rover lurched, almost colliding with one of the main-gate support posts, but McBride fought the wheel and dragged the vehicle back on course.

Bolan swung the Browning in a full circle, facing back toward the compound as the Land Rover sped out across the open, naked Chandran plain. Tilting the barrel up, he raked the active sentry tower, the sustained stream of shells tearing the wooden frame apart. The warrior peered through the dust cloud raised by the vehicle, watching the compound shrink behind them. A secondary explosion sent more flame and smoke into the rapidly darkening sky, highlighting the details of the buildings and the figures running back and forth in confusion and panic.

He leaned his weight on the machine gun, feeling the tension drain from him. It would be easy to let his guard down now, to believe that it was all over and they were free and clear.

He knew different.

Mdofa and his mercenaries would regroup in a very short time, count their losses and realize they might still yet come out ahead of the game. All that stood between them and the success of their planned coup were two people—Kelly McBride and Mack Bolan.

This was Mdofa's country. He would know every rock and every hiding place. He also had the men and the weapons to mount a strong pursuit. There was no doubt that he would do just that, because Lenard Mdofa had a need to win, to become lord and master in his own country. His need was all-consuming, and to save face he couldn't allow himself to be defeated by a single man and woman. Mdofa would instigate an all-out hunt for Bolan and McBride.

Trackers would be sent to hunt them, as well as mechanized vehicles. It would be an undeclared race between the ancient and the modern, to see which fared better against the enemy.

As the Land Rover sped across the flat, exposed terrain, moving farther and farther away from the isolated base, Bolan stared into the deepening gloom and wondered how quickly the dusty, barren Chandran landscape would be turned into the plains of death.

16

It was only as he climbed into the passenger seat beside his companion that Bolan saw the glistening bloody patch on her left shoulder.

"Let's stop here," he said.

McBride eased the Land Rover to a halt, killed the engine and slumped back in her seat.

"Why didn't you tell me?" Bolan asked gruffly.

"You had your hands full."

The warrior peeled her shirt away and examined the wound. The bullet had gouged the top of her shoulder, leaving a raw, open wound. He searched the Land Rover's glove compartment and located a first-aid kit, which he opened. Its contents were basic, but he found antiseptic to clean the wound. McBride gasped when the liquid seeped into the open flesh, despite Bolan's gentle touch. He cleaned the gash and dressed it, applying a bandage and adhesive tape.

"It's going to be sore for a while," he told her as he packed away the kit.

They changed places, with Bolan taking the wheel. He drove into the enveloping darkness. He would have preferred to keep moving during the night, but couldn't risk putting on the headlights in case they were spotted. Driving blind was one way to damage the vehicle and possibly injure himself and his companion. After almost three-quarters of an hour he decided to halt for a while and wait to see if moonlight offered enough illumination to drive by. It would also give them a chance to rest.

McBride had drifted into a restless sleep. Bolan left her while he did an equipment-and-weapons check. There were two jerricans attached to the rear of the Land Rover. Both were fuel containers, and one was full. The other had caught a bullet during their breakout from the compound and had drained itself of fuel. He found two boxes that contained ammo belts for the Browning. There were half a dozen flares for the signal gun, located in a container between the seats, next to the rack holding a pair of Franchi SPAS combat shotguns. Both weapons were fully loaded, and another container was full of cartridges for the assault weapons. Bolan still had the AK-74 with a nearly full magazine and a spare, and he and Kelly both carried a handgun.

There was no food anywhere on the Land Rover, or drinking water. That could prove a problem once dawn brought the sunlight. There weren't any maps or charts. Searching through the glove compartment, Bolan found a large folding knife. He slipped it into one of the blacksuit's zip pockets.

Taking the AK-74, Bolan moved out of the hollow and scouted the area. The moon *was* rising, casting a pale, cold glow across the flat plain. It was totally unknown territory as far as Bolan was concerned, leaving him at a disadvantage in knowing which direction to take. Traveling blind could take him right into the hands of the enemy.

The Executioner needed to be in command of the situation. To function he required a basic knowledge of the territory he was in. With that he could at least plan some kind of strategy.

The way he had been brought into Chandra had denied him any intel on the country. His knowledge about the country had been gained from information he had read, or seen on television. He knew it lay on the east coast of the continent, within the area known as the Horn of Africa. The Horn encompassed a vast tract of land, broken into numerous independent states, and during a long and tragic period those nations, large and small, had suffered wars, drought and famine. Thousands had died. They were still dying.

While the political wrangles over territory and tribal rights went on, and countless stumbling blocks were placed before those trying to help, the innocents still died. They were shot and bombed, starved. They were racked with disease and malnutrition. The affluent nations were fed endless shots of hopeless faces, emaciated bodies and daily death via the television news programs. Reporters, posing before the shriveled walking skeletons, mouthed their platitudes and tried to make their audiences feel the guilt. And while this went on, the warlords terrorized the aid workers and blatantly stole the food shipped in via the relief organizations.

Chandra was one of those states. Colonized by the French and the British, it finally achieved independence in the late seventies. Since then it had been plagued by tribal wars, a dictatorship, then finally a democratic election giving the country over to Victor Joffi. He was struggling to bring his nation stability and to maintain some kind of economic growth. With warlords who continued to fight, and with growing mistrust between the widespread clans, Joffi had his hands full. The last thing he needed, Bolan knew, was the chaos and unrest that Mdofa's planned coup would create.

All that stood between Mdofa and the execution of his plan was Mack Bolan.

The implication struck Bolan as he scanned the desolate plain spreading out around him. On his shoulders rested the knowledge of Mdofa's coup. If he could reach Victor Joffi and warn him, perhaps the Chandran president could withstand the attack Mdofa was going to launch.

Bolan had, by being brought into the country, been given the opportunity to cancel out Mdofa's conspiracy.

It would be somewhat ironic if he carried it off. If he and Kelly had been killed back in Rotterdam, then Mdofa's secret would have died with them. By smuggling them into the country, with the intention of interrogating them, Mdofa had unwittingly presented Bolan with the chance to interfere in his scheme.

The warrior returned to the Land Rover. As gently as he could he woke Kelly. She opened her eyes and grumbled at him, but when he told her what he was planning she became fully awake.

"When they brought you from the landing strip," Bolan said, "did you recognize where you were? Any landmarks?"

McBride thought for a while, then finally shook her head.

"Sorry, Mike. I was still groggy from those injections. The only thing I could say with reasonable certainty was that I think we were near the coast. I could smell the sea on the breeze."

"Did you move along the coast or away?"

"Come to think of it, the smell vanished after a while. So I'd say we must have moved inland."

"How long was the journey?"

"That I can remember. I thought it would never end. We must have been traveling for at least four hours. Maybe five."

"Good. I heard them say they'd brought us in by different routes. My trip lasted around three hours. So they must have brought me by a shorter route."

"Does that help?"

"Gives us some rough distances from the coast. A point of reference."

"What are you planning?" McBride asked, suspicion in her voice.

He glanced at her, unable to restrain a smile.

"To get us out of here."

She shook her head. "There's more to it than that."

"I need to reach Victor Joffi before Mdofa and his hired guns do."

"Mike, that's crazy. Surely Mdofa will be thinking the same thing. He'll have the country covered in every direction. You'll never get through. You can—"

"Kelly, I have to try. You said yourself that Joffi is the only chance Chandra has. If Mdofa topples him, this place is going to fall apart faster than it already is."

"I understand that. But why you, Mike?"

"Charlie Diel pointed the way. Mdofa involved me when he set this in motion."

"And?"

"José Contreros is part of it. This country already has drought and famine. The last thing they need is Contreros and his suppliers creating more misery. It wouldn't stop there. Once the Colombians get a foothold they won't look back."

McBride slumped back in the seat, staring out over the dark plain. She seemed to have something on her mind. She turned to stare at Bolan.

"Is this all really happening, Mike? Sitting here, in the middle of nowhere, I start to think I must be dreaming. I should be back in my apartment in nice cold, wet Amsterdam. Not perched in a Land Rover in Africa, with a bullet wound in my shoulder and a rebel army looking for me."

Bolan held up a hand for silence. He moved away from the Land Rover, walked to the rim of the hollow and scanned the area. He caught the distant, rising sound of an engine. The warrior crawled to the other side of the hollow and stared into the pale night. The sound of the vehicle was becoming louder. It was definitely coming their way. He judged it to be no more than a quarter mile off. It also seemed to be on a direct path to the hollow.

Someone had to have picked up on their tire tracks.

He returned to the Land Rover.

McBride had unlimbered one of the shotguns and had the weapon resting across her lap.

"Have they found us?" she asked.

"We'll know soon enough."

"Do we stay put or make a run for it?"

The Executioner had already considered that. If they ran they would be out in the open with nowhere to hide, and unaware of how many other vehicles might be lying in wait for such a move.

The alternative was to stay put and hope they could take out the approaching trackers.

Either way involved a risk.

But if Bolan could silence the oncoming enemy they might gain themselves some extra time.

He glanced at McBride. "We stay put."

17

The approaching vehicle halted. The motor died.

Mack Bolan, flat on the ground and armed only with his knife, waited in silence.

He had vacated the hollow and concealed himself yards away in the scant cover of tangled brush. McBride lay beneath the parked Land Rover, armed with one of the SPAS shotguns. Bolan hoped there would be no need for her to use the weapon. His intention was to deal with the trackers silently.

The soft sounds of their approach came after a few minutes. Bolan discerned two of them. They were about twenty feet apart, approaching the hollow from different angles, and they were moving very quietly.

He spotted the closer man as the guy paused and crouched, his head moving from side to side as he checked out the area. He was lean and had a shaved head, his black skin gleaming like polished ebony in the moonlight. The man was clad in camou gear and carried a suppressed Uzi.

Bolan watched the man, sensing that he was uneasy about moving on. Something was making him hold back. He turned and looked across the apparently empty plain. His right arm lifted, his hand making a short, chopping motion. He was warning his partner to halt, too. The man stood. He was tall, holding himself erect. He began to turn, his head angled slightly forward as he inspected the area minutely.

Gripping the wood handle of his knife, Bolan began to wriggle backward, away from his hiding place. He slid into the deeper shadows beyond the brush, his blacksuit helping to conceal his outline.

The tall African moved into action. He was already facing Bolan's direction, and with the speed of a striking snake he darted forward, swinging around the Uzi. The suppressed autoweapon spit out a stream of 9 mm slugs. They lashed into the brush where Bolan had been hiding only seconds earlier, shredding the vegetation. The African continued his forward motion, the Uzi tracking in on the brush.

Bolan, by this time, was on his feet. He had commenced his attack the moment the African had opened fire. Powering into a hard run, he had circled, coming in from the African's left side, and he was on the gunner before the man could react. The warrior hit the African from the side, his shoulder slamming into his ribs. The African was stunned momentarily. Bolan hooked his left leg behind the guy's knees, hammered him across the chest with his left arm and dropped him to the ground. The warrior straddled his adversary's chest and drove the knife deep into his heart, silencing him forever.

The Executioner heard a soft sound. He reached out and grabbed the dead man's Uzi. He rolled away from the body and stretched prone on the ground.

A hushed voice reached him, questioning, demanding a reply. Bolan pinpointed the source. Now he could see a second man, more stockily built, with wide shoulders. It was a white man, his face smeared with camou paint. He was half-crouched, searching the shadows as he advanced. He also carried a suppressed Uzi.

Bolan calculated range, went up onto one knee and waited until the man was looking in the opposite direction. The warrior stroked the trigger and fired a short burst that drilled the man in the upper chest. He grunted once, arms flying wide as he went over on his back, heels drumming frantically against the hard ground as he died.

The warrior retreated into the darkness, searching for the vehicle the men had arrived in. He found it two hundred yards away. Crouching in the shadows of a thicket, Bolan checked out the vehicle. It was empty. No backup man waited. He closed on the vehicle silently, still cautious, until he was satisfied he was alone.

The vehicle was an open Land Rover equipped for fast travel. It carried no surplus weight other than a single can of fuel. Behind the seats Bolan found a rucksack containing rations, and a couple of sleeping bags. He took them, and the two canteens of water.

Shouldering the fuel can, Bolan returned to the hollow, softly calling to Kelly. She wriggled out from under the Land Rover, slapping dust from her clothing.

"I'll never be clean again," she muttered.

"Here," Bolan said, handing her one of the canteens.

She opened the canteen and moistened her lips, savoring the water. Then she took a small swallow, watching as Bolan loaded the gear into the back of their vehicle. He emptied the fuel into the tank of the Land Rover.

Bolan made his way back to where the two dead men lay. He took their weapons and retrieved his knife from the African's chest. He wiped the blade, closed the heavy knife and dropped it back into his pocket. The African wore a web belt around his waist that held a large, sheathed knife. Bolan freed the belt and looped it around his own waist.

McBride made no comment as he loaded the weapons into the Land Rover, then slid behind the wheel. She knew what he had had to do in order to gain the weapons and equipment. She slid into the passenger seat, locking the SPAS back in the rack as Bolan started the vehicle and eased it out of the hollow.

"If we can keep the moon behind us, it means we're moving roughly to the east. Should take us toward the coast. If we're lucky we might find habitation."

"If Mdofa doesn't find us first," McBride reminded him.

"I hadn't forgotten."

Bolan picked up one of the canteens and eased off the cap. Taking a swallow, he rinsed out his dry mouth.

The Executioner wasn't fooling himself. They would be extremely lucky to reach the coast without encountering more of Mdofa's men.

He turned the Land Rover east, driving steadily to keep the engine noise to a minimum. Using the silvery light of the moon, Bolan kept an eye open for any other movement around them. He hadn't forgotten about Mdofa's two helicopters and checked the sky, as well. Every half hour he halted, taking the opportunity to make a thorough search of the terrain, listening for distant sounds that might offer him some indication that Mdofa's people were in the area.

According to his watch, they had been traveling for three hours. The temperature had dropped considerably, the night air holding a definite chill. Bolan had unrolled the sleeping bags and wrapped one around Kelly. She had stirred restlessly, but hadn't wakened. She had fallen asleep soon after they had moved off, and Bolan had allowed her to rest. Her shoulder was hurting, the pain nagging at her, and sleep was the best option.

Bolan went EVA with the AK-74 and circled the area. Nothing stirred. The only sound came from some distant animal. Once again beside the Land Rover, the warrior lifted one of the canteens and took a slow swallow. He opened one of the rucksacks and took out a bar of dried fruit. Chewing on it, he raised his head as a cool breeze wafted by.

Minutes later, as Bolan prepared to move on, he realized that the breeze was becoming stronger. Now he could hear the distant sound of the wind. It was coming from the east, blowing inland from the sea. Stowing away the rucksack, he felt the gritty patter of dust against his back. He turned to face the wind and could feel its increasing strength. He tasted dry dust in the air, and it rattled against the side of the Land Rover as he drove off. The warrior could make out the rolling dust clouds that were being driven before the oncoming wind.

There was a storm coming, a full-blown storm of driving, choking dust that would sweep across the flat plain with nothing to stop it. There was no way to avoid it, no protection, no defence.

And Mack Bolan was heading straight into it.

18

The storm hit within the half hour. Gritty dust lashed at the Land Rover, striking the windshield with a harsh sound. The force of the wind rocked the vehicle, and Bolan was forced to hang on to the wheel with both hands.

He was making little headway now. The moonlit night sky was obscured by the swirling fog of dust. Bolan found he could barely see farther than the front of the Land Rover. He couldn't be sure what lay ahead.

He was sure of one thing, though—he was lost.

For all he knew he was way off course. He could have been going in circles. The thick clouds of dust driving across the empty plain shut him off from any tangible point of reference he might guide himself by. Bolan was forced to reduce his pace to less than a walk. Peering through the dust-lashed windshield, he was forced to accept he couldn't see where he was going.

The Land Rover's engine began to falter. He teased the gas pedal, trying to coax life back into the weakening power unit. It steadied for a short time, then began to run raggedly again, refusing to respond to his coaxing. Spluttering and coughing, it died completely. With a final lurch the vehicle ground to a halt. Bolan tried to start it again. The engine turned over but refused to fire. He flicked off the ignition and sat back in resignation. For the time being this was where they were going to have to stay.

Kelly was still asleep, restlessly moving in her seat. Leaning across, Bolan adjusted the sleeping bag around her. He unrolled the other one and covered himself with it, turning his face away from the drifting dust that was creeping around the windshield. Open Land Rovers, with no doors or tops, were fine in calm, clear weather. They got no points from Bolan where dust storms were concerned.

The Uzi lay across the warrior's lap beneath the sleeping bag. He wasn't expecting any visitors, but past experience had inbred total caution within him. It had kept him alive through many desperate encounters, and his actions had become automatic when it came to survival.

The sound of the storm lulled him, the mournful drone rising and falling, accompanied by the hiss and rattle of the gritty dust as it was blown over the plain. Bolan's body, weary from the relentless pace of the recent past, began to relax. Fatigue finally took over. Bolan drifted into a shallow sleep, his eyes opening regularly, but he saw nothing, heard nothing, other than the howl of the storm and the seemingly eternal darkness created by the drifting dust.

THE SILENCE EVENTUALLY woke him. Bolan opened one eye and surveyed the early brightness of dawn. Warm sunlight touched the side of his face. He moved, feeling the binding stiffness in his joints from sleeping on the uncomfortable seat of the Land Rover. The sleeping bag dropped away from his body with a dry hiss of layered dust. He looked around, seeing only the same empty, featureless plain stretching in all directions.

Bolan searched the floor of the vehicle until he located one of the canteens. He uncapped it, rinsed out his dry mouth, then took a drink. The water was warm and flat, but Bolan was in no condition to complain. He swung his legs to the ground, pulling himself upright, feeling his joints protest. With the Uzi clutched in his left hand he took a couple of steps away from the Land Rover, arching his back. His face felt stiff, too. Touching it, he could feel the taut bruises from Dekker's beating.

The warrior spent a few minutes moving around, stretching gently until he felt comfortable. He turned to look over the Land Rover and saw that the front was almost completely buried by drifted dust. He recalled the sound it had made the night before, grinding to a halt. Dust had to have gotten inside the filter system, maybe even into the fuel. If that was the case, he'd have no success starting the vehicle. On an impulse he checked the Land Rover for a toolbox. Other than a jack, there was nothing he could use to strip down any parts. Even if he did, there was no guarantee he could get the vehicle running again. If dust had gotten inside the engine, he would need fresh filters, or an air line to clean out the grit from difficult sections.

The other thing he was short of was time. Mdofa would certainly have more men searching for them.

Bolan began to organize the equipment and weapons for moving out. The only answer was for him and Kelly to start out on foot.

He took the two canteens, then put the first-aid kit and the extra cartridges for the SPAS shotgun into the rucksack. He decided to take the AK-74 and the two handguns, as well. Rolling up the sleeping bag he'd used, the warrior strapped it to the side of the rucksack. He woke Kelly, leaving her to come around while he made use of the sleeping bag she'd slept in. By the time she had roused herself fully, Bolan was kneeling beside the Land Rover, cutting up the sleeping bag.

"This for us?" she asked.

Bolan nodded, concentrating on cutting the outer fabric of the sleeping bag into two large squares. Placing them aside, he then cut long strips and twisted them to form crude ties. The thick insulation from inside the sleeping bag was fashioned into a couple of pads. These were laid on top of the head, with the large squares folded diagonally and placed over the top, with the excess of the material allowed to fall down over the neck and shoulders. The arrangement was based on the traditional Arab headdress. The rough ties went around the head to hold the material in place. Bolan had also allowed enough material so that a fold could be pulled across the face to protect the mouth and nose.

After he had fixed two headdresses Bolan shrugged into the rucksack and adjusted the straps.

"We going for a walk?" she asked.

"We had a little blow last night while you were asleep," Bolan said. "The Rover isn't going any farther, but we are. How's the shoulder?"

"Sore and stiff. But it isn't hurting as much."

He handed her the SPAS shotgun, which she carried over her good shoulder by the sling.

They moved off without further comment, heading east toward the rising sun.

They trudged across the dusty, featureless plain for almost fifteen minutes before McBride broke the silence.

"Mike, how far did we get last night?" she asked.

"Three, four hours before the storm hit. After that it's hard to say. I kept moving as long as I could. During the storm, I couldn't be certain I was going in the right direction. When the engine stalled I called it a day."

Bolan cradled the AK-74 across his body as he walked. He maintained a steady pace without putting too much strain on them. The going would become harder once the sun rose fully. Then they would have to be careful not to allow too much body moisture to be lost. The trick was to drink enough water to replace that lost, but not in excess. Travel in arid, open country was a fine balancing act—being aware of the land and the climate, maintaining a sensible pace and respecting the strictures of the environment.

Through eyes narrowed against the hard glare of the strengthening sun, Bolan checked out the terrain. Mdofa's people would have been delayed by the storm, too, but by now he expected them to be on the prowl again, searching for the two fugitives, sweeping back and forth in regular patterns.

Sooner or later they would make contact.

THE SILENCE WAS BROKEN by a distant pulse of sound.

Bolan paused, listening. The sound faded, then returned. It was above and behind them. He turned, scanning the cloudless, empty sky.

"Mike?"

Bolan didn't answer. He was watching a far-off dark spot that was heading their way. The glare of the bright sky hurt his eyes. He narrowed them, focusing on the spot, and saw that it was beginning to form into a recognizable shape—a helicopter.

It was flying on a course that suggested it was following their line of travel from the abandoned Land Rover.

He gestured for Kelly to follow him and led the way to where a thin line of brush straggled across the plain. It was the only cover visible.

The chopping sound of the helicopter filled the air.

Bolan pushed his companion to the sandy earth. He burrowed himself close by, feeling the scratchy brush tug at his clothing. He pulled the trailing surplus cloth of the headdress over his mouth and nose to keep out the dust, tucking the end into the headband. Then he pulled the AK-74 into position and waited.

The helicopter dropped to within ten feet of the ground, hovering impatiently, the rotorwash stirring up clouds of dust. It was no more than thirty feet from the brush thicket. The aircraft was the small two-seater machine, not the massive Hind gunship. Even so, it presented a threat. Despite the dust swirling around the chopper, Bolan spotted the light machine gun suspended from a swivel, jutting from the passenger access. The door had been removed to accommodate the weapon. A man clad in camou gear sat behind the gun, studying the ground, conversing with the pilot via a throat microphone. Something seemed to have drawn his attention. He kept pointing groundward, agitated.

Bolan gripped the AK-74, his finger curling against the trigger as the helicopter sank closer to the ground. The machine gunner unbuckled his harness and reached behind him for an assault rifle. He exited the cockpit and stood on the skid a moment before jumping to the ground. As he landed, the helicopter rose to around fifty feet, hovering noisily.

The man on the ground was one of Liam Redland's mercs. He backtracked, picking up the trail Bolan and McBride had left some thirty feet from his landing position. There the footprints were clear, undisturbed by the rotorwash. The merc crouched, inspecting the prints, turning to follow them as they proceeded eastward. His eye came to rest on the brush where Bolan and McBride lay. He stayed in his crouch, staring at the thicket, and McBride could almost read what was going through his mind.

The merc raised his rifle, tracking in on the brush, and triggered a burst.

Dirt geysered into the air as the slugs plowed into the ground, mere inches to Bolan's right. He ducked his head, feeling the grit pepper his body. Pulling his knees under him, the warrior powered up off the ground, his eyes searching for the now-retreating merc, his AK-74 swinging into the firing position.

Overhead the chopper began a tight swing, losing altitude as the pilot maneuvered to block Bolan off from his partner. The aircraft dropped swiftly, raising a choking cloud of dust.

Bolan ducked to a crouch as the helicopter swooped in over his head. The roar of the engine deafened him, and he felt himself being dragged across the ground by the suction of the rotors. He threw out his free hand, digging his fingers in the earth to stall his slide.

Dimly he heard a thump of sound, followed by another and another. The helicopter drifted away, still low, but moving away from him. Bolan felt the pressure lessen and he gathered his legs under him, returning to his hunt for the merc, aware that he would still be around.

The boom of a shot came from his left, and it wasn't aimed at Bolan.

The warrior realized that the merc was shooting at Kelly. The woman had fired on the helicopter and drawn the hardman's attention.

As the dust began to clear, Bolan made out the hazy shape of the merc. The guy pegged Bolan at the same time, and each man brought his weapon into play.

Blinking the grit from his eyes, the Executioner tracked in with the AK-74, stroking the trigger as he saw the merc run forward, trying to bring his rifle to his shoulder. Bolan's shot caught the man in the upper left thigh, tearing a bloody hole in the flesh. The merc gave a pained grunt, then collapsed to the ground, rolling and scrambling to his feet again. He worked the trigger of the assault rifle and fired a stream of slugs in Bolan's direction.

The warrior was on the move himself, weaving as he closed in, and he felt the thud of the slugs as they pounded the dry earth around him. He paused long enough to center the merc in his sights, then touched the trigger of the AK-74.

The hardman was stopped in his tracks as Bolan's burst took him dead-center in the chest. He fell back, his body held rigid in shock. By the time the Executioner reached his adversary, the man was dead. Bolan recognized his face immediately; he had been one of the men who had been with Dekker when Bolan had regained consciousness in the hut at the airstrip.

The dead man carried a number of fragmentation grenades on his combat harness. Bolan snatched a couple free before he ducked away from the body as the helicopter made a dangerously low sweep at him. The warrior hugged the earth, the roar of the chopper's engine shutting out every other sound. Then it was pulling away, banking as the pilot made a tight turn.

Bolan was up and running, with no place to hide. The open plain gave all the advantage to the pilot.

The flyer took his chopper in low, turning it sideways toward Bolan, letting it drift in at him. The bulk of the aircraft loomed large in the warrior's vision. He knew that the pilot was trying to hit him with the skid. If the pilot could keep it up for long enough, he might eventually tire his quarry and be able to overcome him.

The pilot, in his determination to get to the man who had killed his partner, had forgotten about Kelly McBride. She edged out of the thicket, keeping to the pilot's blind side, then opened fire again with the SPAS. Her third shot struck the plastic canopy. The pilot, distracted, lost his momentum for a few seconds, which was enough for Bolan to respond.

He yanked out the pin from one of the grenades and released the lever. Counting off the seconds, he lobbed the bomb through the open side of the canopy, then turned away and began to distance himself from the chopper.

The remaining seconds ticked away.

The grenade detonated, blowing out the canopy and the pilot. The stricken helicopter dropped like a stone and struck the ground with a crash of tortured metal.

Bolan kept moving, waving McBride back.

Somewhere within the stricken helicopter leaking fuel and flashing sparks came together. Vapor ignited, and in turn so did the bulk of the fuel. The sudden ball of fire was accompanied by a heavy thump of sound. The crumpled wreck vanished in the swelling boil of flame. Smoke rose in a dark spiral, staining the blue sky.

"This is getting to be a habit," McBride commented.

Bolan crossed to the dead merc and removed the combat harness. He put it on and secured the grenade he'd snatched.

With a gesture to McBride, he continued the slow trek east.

19

By nightfall they had covered roughly fifteen miles. By strictly rationing the water they carried, using it only to compensate moisture lost due to sweating, they were able to maintain body equilibrium. They rested at midday, finding a shallow depression and utilizing the remaining sleeping bag to shade them. When darkness came and the temperature began to fall, they rested again for a couple of hours before continuing. They used the moonlight to guide them, sharing the scant rations Bolan had found in the rucksack as they walked along.

By midnight they reached a low range of hills, where they found stronger growths of vegetation. Bolan located a snug hiding place beneath a shelf of weathered stone. He shrugged out of the rucksack and spread the sleeping bag for Kelly.

He made her sit so he could check her shoulder. The wound was still sore, but it looked healthy. Bolan cleaned and redressed it.

"Where are you going to sleep?" she asked.

"I'll manage."

"Meaning you're going to sit up all night keeping watch. That's crazy. You need rest, too. Unless you want to start falling over tomorrow."

"I can catch a few winks once I've checked the area."

McBride was going to protest further, but she saw it would do no good. So she turned in.

Bolan scouted the immediate area. It looked clear, but he was still uneasy about the fact that there had been no contact with Mdofa's people since the helicopter incident. If they were out, then someone had to have seen the smoke from the burning chopper.

So why were they holding back? Had Mdofa decided on another approach?

Perhaps he was pulling in his people and moving them ahead of Bolan. Maybe the idea was to have them lie in wait for Bolan if he got through to the coast and possible contact with the authorities.

The many thoughts whirling around in Bolan's tired mind only increased his physical weariness. He knew what Kelly had said was true, and sensible. He did need some rest. Dawn would bring another day of soaring temperatures and possible confrontation with Mdofa's force. He would need to be fully alert then. Now was the time to take advantage of a lull in the hostilities.

He made another wide sweep, patiently checking and rechecking, listening and looking.

Nothing.

KELLY STIRRED as Bolan eased beneath the overhang. When he rested his rifle against the rock and put his back to it, she raised her head.

"What are you doing?"

"What you suggested. Taking a rest."

"Sitting there in the cold?"

"I'm fine."

"Well, I'm not, Belasko, so get your butt under this sleeping bag. It's cold."

She pressed against him, her supple body molding to his. In another place and time the contact would have been more than desirable. In their present circumstances it was merely welcomed. Bolan eased his arm around Kelly's shoulders and she leaned her weight against him. Her hands slid over his taut body, drawing him close.

"What is this?"

"It's called a parang. A large knife."

"It certainly is."

"Go to sleep."

"Good night, Mike."

THEY FINISHED the last of the food in the rucksack, drank a little more of their dwindling water and watched as the sun came up and the chill of the night dissipated with the rising heat.

From the top of the low hills, they were able to see the lay of the land ahead of them. The endless plain they had previously been crossing had begun to break up. There was more vegetation, and rock formations like lonely islands dotted the landscape.

"Looks promising," McBride commented, "and maybe familiar."

Bolan glanced up from adjusting his headdress.

"You know this area?"

"I might. I'll be able to tell you better when we get down there. It looks different from up here."

Pulling on the rucksack, the warrior picked up his rifle and waited while McBride fixed her own head-dress.

He led the way down the far side of the range of hills. As they descended they picked up the scent of the vegetation. Reaching level ground, they were even able to pick out colorful patches of flowers among the thickets.

Bolan paused at a growth of broad-leaved plants. He ran his hand across the greenery, and it came away moist.

"Condensation," he said. "Could mean we're closer to the coast than we think."

McBride took a deep breath. "The air's not so dry. Mike, if I'm right and I do know this area, then we're definitely nearer the coast."

Bolan moistened his fingers again, touching them to his lips. "Slightly salty. Cool air from the sea drifting inland as the heat builds, probably as mist."

He walked on, McBride trailing behind. They came across the dry, cracked bed of a meandering water-course. The shallow banks were crumbling, the soil parched. The scant grasses that grew there were with-ered and brown. McBride paused, checking the snak-ing pattern of the riverbed.

"We should keep heading east. Mike, I'm certain there's a village a few miles distant. It's one we deliv-ered supplies to."

Before moving out, Bolan ran a quick weapons check. Satisfied, he led the way along the riverbed.

As THEY CRAWLED over the dusty slope, Bolan looked over the crest and scanned the untidy sprawl of crude huts that was the isolated village Kelly had described to him. It lay close to the dry riverbed they had been following. A few twisted, scrawny trees edged the bank, providing meager shade from the sun.

It was close to noon, and the heat was overpowering. Bolan felt drained, despite having deliberately slowed their pace. The water they carried was almost gone. Kelly was resting in the shade of a dusty thicket nearby. Her reserves had finally given out, and Bolan had insisted she wait while he checked out the village.

There was some movement around the huts. People went about their business. Smoke spiraled lazily into the sky from cooking fires. Bolan lay still and studied the village for a long time. It looked innocent enough, but when it came down to it, that was how a setup was supposed to appear.

If Bolan had been on his own, he would have given the village a miss. Kelly's presence and her condition made it vital he get her some help. He hadn't told her yet, but he intended to continue on alone. Matters were becoming urgent now. He needed to get through to Victor Joffi as soon as he could.

Moving along the crest, the Executioner followed it down to the dry riverbed. He used the crumbling bank as cover as he worked his way toward the village. The tree line provided extra cover, enabling him to survey the activity around the huts.

He was able to discern the poor physical condition of the occupants. Those he could see were thin, the flesh hanging from their bones. Deep-sunken eyes stared out from gaunt faces. They moved around slowly, almost without purpose. These people would offer no challenge to someone like Lenard Mdofa. If he came to power, there would be little resistance if this village represented the state of the country. The villagers had enough to do trying to stay alive from day to day.

The Executioner edged forward, clearing the tree line and sprinting to the rear wall of the closest hut. He crept around the perimeter of the flimsy building so that he could see more of the village layout.

Looking across the open area that served as the village square, Bolan checked out the huts on the opposite side.

The first thing he saw was a Land Rover, parked tightly between two of the huts. It had a two-man crew. The guy lounging behind the wheel looked like one of Liam Redland's mercs. His partner was a powerful African, slumped against the Rover's front fender. Bolan watched them for a few minutes, and they gave the impression of having been in position for some time. The heat and the boredom were starting to get to them. It showed in their attitude, the way they were relaxing rather than paying attention to the job.

Bolan didn't take for granted that there were only two men. It was possible others might be inside the huts. One way or another he was going to have to deal with them. The two by the Land Rover would need to be handled quietly.

He moved along the rear of the huts until he reached the last one. At this end of the village were crude pens, constructed from weathered, spindly poles, intended to contain the village's livestock. The pens were empty now. From their condition it was plain they hadn't been used for some time. Bolan bellied down and edged his way along the rear of the pens. At the far corner he gauged the distance between himself and the first of the huts on the other side of the village.

Movement close by caught the warrior's attention. He watched as a skeletal dog wandered in his direction to stand eyeing him. The animal appeared more curious than aggressive. Flies hovered around it, crawling over the open sores that marked its body and limbs. Bolan held his position until the animal tired and wandered away.

Gathering himself, Bolan made the short dash to the cover of the closest hut. Pressed against the flimsy wall, he could hear the tired murmur of voices. A child was crying. It was the thin, wasted wail of starvation, the sound of a youngster too weak to do anything else but express its distress. The sound tugged at Bolan's emotions. He felt for these people. They were slowly dying, through no fault of their own, and the hardest thing to listen to was the cry of the most vulnerable.

His thoughts swung to Lenard Mdofa, planning the continued deprivation of his own nation simply so he could rise to power. The man's ambition would be built over the bones of these people. He would toast his victory in luxury while ignoring the cries of hungry children.

That thought more than anything spurred Bolan on along the huts, until he reached the place where the Land Rover sat with its armed passengers.

Peering around the rear wall of the hut, the warrior saw the white merc behind the wheel pick up a handset.

"Rover 4 to Control. Come in Control. Over." A pause, then, "No, not a damn thing. How the hell do I know? Maybe they went a different way. Over." After another long pause, the merc became increasingly annoyed. "Look, I don't give a damn about that. We're here in the middle of this stinking village like a pair of prize assholes. As far as I'm concerned they're not coming here. I'm keeping to the schedule. We give it one more hour, then we move out and pick up the next location. Yeah? Well, tell Mdofa he's really scaring me. I'm sittin' here peein' my damn pants. Rover 4, over and out!"

The merc slammed down the handset. He dragged himself out of the Land Rover, searching his pockets for a cigarette, muttering darkly when he found he was out.

"Hey, you got a smoke, Oku?" he asked.

The African produced a crumpled pack and handed them over. The merc fished one out and lighted it, coughing harshly on the smoke.

"What the hell do you guys put in these, elephant dung?"

The African laughed, shaking his head.

"You got no stomach, man."

"Damn well won't have if I smoke many of these," the merc complained.

He turned around and came face-to-face with Mack Bolan.

The merc's hand dropped to the autopistol holstered on his right hip.

Bolan drove the butt of the AK-74 into the man's stomach, doubling him over, and as he sagged the warrior kneed him full in the face. Bone cracked and the merc straightened up with a jerk, blood streaming from his crushed nose. Following through, Bolan swung the rifle again, arcing it up beneath the merc's jaw. His head flew back, twisted at an awkward angle as his neck broke. The merc, dead on his feet, slumped backward, colliding with Oku as the big African swung around, alerted by the noise. There was a moment of confusion as Oku hastily shoved the corpse aside and tried to bring his own weapon into play.

Bolan swung the assault rifle at Oku's head. The African grunted in pain and pawed at the glinting barrel of the rifle. Bolan hit him again, and this time Oku stumbled. A final blow to the base of the skull pitched Oku facedown in the dust.

The Executioner stepped around the downed man. As he did a massive hand shot out and gripped his ankle. Bolan felt a savage pull and he was dragged off his feet. He landed hard, the AK-74 bouncing from his hand. A dark shadow covered him as Oku threw himself on top of Bolan, straddling him, his great hands closing around his adversary's throat, thick fingers digging in deeply. The warrior took in a final breath before Oku's stranglehold shut off his supply. He fought back the urge to panic.

Aware that he had only a short time to act, Bolan brought up both hands and without a moment's hesitation jabbed both thumbs into Oku's eyes, gouging deep into the sockets. The African shook his head in an attempt to stop the pain Bolan was inflicting. The Executioner only pushed harder, feeling his thumbs sinking deeper. His fingers gripped the side of Oku's skull, giving him leverage. Oku gave a roar of agony. He released Bolan's throat and reared back, clutching at his burning eyes.

Using his reprieve, the Executioner arched his body, throwing Oku off. Coming to his knees, Bolan freed the heavy parang from its sheath at his side, turned and sank the curving blade into his opponent's chest. The African crashed over on his back, kicking like a speared fish. Bolan climbed to his feet, rubbing his aching throat.

He picked up the AK-74 and dusted it off as he prepared to move out, intending to check out the rest of the village.

Bolan sensed movement near the front of the Land Rover. He about-faced, and found himself confronted by a group of staring Africans, armed with an assortment of spears, knives and pangas.

20

The obvious leader of the group was a small, round-shouldered man with piercing, bright eyes and a healthier appearance than his companions. He looked from Bolan to the dead men and back again.

"You have killed them both," he said matter-of-factly, "so you must be the one they came looking for."

He peered beyond where Bolan stood, his eyes searching the shadows.

"Where is the woman?"

"Resting. We've walked a long way across the plain. She needs help."

"Tell me why we should help you."

"The woman is Kelly McBride. She works for the relief organization that sends you food and medical supplies. Now she needs your help."

"Are you telling me the truth?"

Bolan nodded.

"Then take me to her."

The warrior climbed into the Land Rover, fired up the engine and waited as the African settled in the passenger seat. Dropping the vehicle into gear, Bolan wheeled the Land Rover out from between the huts and through the village. He gunned it across the open ground and up the slope. Braking, he stepped out and crossed to where McBride lay. Crouching beside her, he eased the headdress off, exposing her tangled red hair, and heard a gasp of astonishment from the African.

"It is McBride."

Bolan stood and held out his hand.

"I'm Mike Belasko."

The African grasped Bolan's hand with his own.

"I am Matthias Obotu. You are welcome, Belasko."

Between them they carried McBride to the Land Rover, placing her in the rear where Obotu fussed over her like a mother hen. Bolan drove back to the village. Even before they entered, the African was announcing their arrival by yelling out McBride's name. A crowd quickly gathered, following the Land Rover's progress to the village square.

Once the Executioner drew to a stop, Obotu organized matters. McBride was helped into one of the huts, and several of the younger women went in to tend to her.

"They will look after her," Obotu stated. "You must tell me what has happened."

"First tell me something."

"What is that?"

"When I first saw you with the other men, you were all armed. Why?"

"We had decided to confront the intruders to tell them they would have to leave. The women and children were frightened. They are already weak and not certain how they will survive. It was not right those men came and threatened us. Told us they would destroy the village if we helped the people they were looking for. We did it out of foolish pride. Our men were once great fighting warriors."

"I'd say they still are," Bolan told him, thinking of how the group of starving, sickly men carrying primitive weapons had been ready for a confrontation with a pair of mercenaries armed with the latest in modern armament.

Smiling with pride, Obotu took Bolan to one of the huts and led him inside. The hut was almost bare, containing little more than crude, handmade furniture and a small cooking stove in one corner. Obotu brought tin mugs that he had filled with strong tea from a steaming pot. The warrior took his mug and squatted on the hard-packed dirt floor, facing his host.

"The men who were here. They worked for Lenard Mdofa. Am I right?"

Bolan nodded. "They've been chasing us ever since we broke out of Mdofa's base."

"What have you done that has upset the man so much?"

"I've learned that he's planning some kind of takeover from Victor Joffi."

Obotu frowned. "Are you saying he wants to kill the president?"

"I'm pretty sure that's what is behind everything."

"I am not surprised. Mdofa has always wanted to be president. But by his own rules. He has also always known that no one in the country would ever vote for him. He is a bad man. He clings to the tribal ways and says he is right to challenge Joffi. Everyone knows they are only words.''

"This is more than a challenge," Bolan said. "Mdofa has been smuggling weapons into the country to arm his men. They have been using the food containers belonging to the Sonderstrom charity, and Mdofa has handpicked white mercenaries on his payroll.''

"I have heard this. On the streets of the city there have been boasts from Mdofa's followers.''

"I'm surprised that the president hasn't heard.''

Obotu shrugged. "Sometimes the leader does not know what goes on at his feet. His head is so full of other matters he hears only what his advisers choose to tell him.''

The African's simple logic rang true in Bolan's ears. Often a leader of government was "protected" against rumor and gossip because those around him decided it was in his best interests not to know. There was also the other side of the coin—distancing the leader from rumor because it was in the interests of the protectors. Sometimes those openly defending the leader were only doing so in order to hide their own disloyalty.

"President Joffi is a good man. Perhaps too good and too trusting. He is trying to help Chandra, but there is too much for him to handle alone.''

"I think Mdofa is out to grab all the prizes for himself and his chosen few," Bolan said.

"Mdofa's greed is for power and power alone. He would not care if we all died.''

"Matthias, he's also planning to go into business with one of the South American cartels to bring addictive drugs to the African continent."

"You know this for a fact?"

Bolan nodded. "The Colombian Mdofa had contact with in Holland is here in Chandra. I saw him at the base."

"You must explain to me how all this came about," the African said, refilling their mugs.

Keeping to the bare bones, Bolan related the chain of events that brought Kelly McBride and himself to Chandra. He brought the African up to date with the breakout from Mdofa's base and their trek across the Chandran plain.

"But you will never reach Joffi. He is well protected by his bodyguards. He never goes anywhere alone. And if what you say is true, then Mdofa will have his people on the streets of the city looking for you. They are bad people, but they are also clever."

Bolan emptied his mug of tea. "Then, Matthias, we'll have to be even smarter."

"I think I am going to like you, Belasko."

"You don't live here all the time, do you?" the warrior asked.

Obotu shook his head. "I spend time in the city to obtain what I can for the village. Sometimes I buy, sometimes I steal. You have seen the people. And the children. We must look out for ourselves. When McBride and her trucks come, we have food for a while. But that soon goes, and we have to wait for the next delivery. So I go to the city and find work of sorts. One day we will prosper. One day it will rain again and we can grow crops and raise our cattle. And soon President Joffi will make his promises come true."

"If Mdofa doesn't get to him first."

Obotu nodded. "Let us make arrangements."

While Obotu went to talk to his people, Bolan visited McBride. As he entered the hut, the village women left silently.

"Hi," she said, trying to appear bright. Her voice, though, sounded tired.

"You were right about the village," Bolan told her.

"Have you met Matthias Obotu?"

"He's quite a character. He's going to help me get to the city."

"Mike, be careful. Mdofa isn't going to give in now. He could be getting desperate."

"You just concentrate on getting some rest."

"Will I be coming with you?"

"As far as the city, yes. I don't want to leave you here in case Mdofa's people come looking."

Obotu entered the hut. He smiled when he saw Kelly.

"It is good to see you, McBride."

"And you, Matthias."

"Belasko, I have spoken with the men of the village. They will take the bodies away and bury them where no one will find them. If Mdofa's people come, they will be told their men have left as they said they would."

"Matthias, make sure no one takes anything from the bodies that might be recognized by Mdofa's people. It could make things very bad for them if anything was found here."

"I will do that now."

When Obotu had left, McBride reached out to touch Bolan's arm.

"Does this mean we've finished having fun together, Mike Belasko?"

He smiled down at her. "Fun? You're a hell of a lady, Kelly McBride."

"You really think so?"

Bolan leaned over and touched her cheek. She stared up at him, her eyes boring deep into his with unconcealed frankness.

"Now do as you're told and rest," he ordered.

Outside he saw that the two bodies had already been moved. A number of the women were arranging blankets in the back of the Land Rover for McBride.

"We can leave as soon as you are ready," Obotu stated.

"How long will it take us to reach the city?" Bolan asked.

"We will go by a trail away from the roads in case Mdofa's people are still looking. We will be in the city before nightfall."

Obotu had made sure that all the weapons had been taken from the bodies. These, along with the two AK-74 rifles, were placed in a storage locker behind the seats.

Helped by the women, McBride walked to the Land Rover. Once she was settled they were ready to go. Bolan climbed behind the wheel with Obotu sitting beside him. The village turned out to watch them go.

"Have you lost many people?" Bolan asked.

"Yes. They die from lack of food, from drinking bad water when they cannot do without, or from no water."

"Have you lost family?"

The little African fell silent for a time. He cleared his throat. "My wife died two years ago, as did the child she was carrying."

Bolan didn't say anything. There was no need. He knew what losing close ones meant. He'd gone through it himself. The losses still hurt. They always would.

NOON CAME AND WENT. The heat was as unrelenting as ever. But at least now, as they moved closer to the coast, there was a slight breeze, occasionally bringing the scent of the sea.

They were moving through countryside that sustained much more vegetation than Bolan had seen since arriving in Chandra. Heavy thickets, stands of trees, patches of grassland—all showed the strain of surviving through a prolonged drought. The plant life was dry and bleached, the grass yellow and brown. The earth that carried the roots was arid and powdery, or baked so hard it had the consistency of iron.

Obotu, true to his word, kept them moving along trails that were all but invisible to Bolan's eye. The way was rough, full of obstacles that would have defeated anyone unfamiliar with the terrain. The African had an intimate knowledge of the land that came from living with and not living on it.

In the early afternoon Obotu raised a hand. Bolan eased off the throttle and brought the Land Rover to a halt. He kept the vehicle in gear, with the engine ticking over.

"Wait a moment, Belasko."

Bolan saw the African lean forward to peer through the dusty, flyspecked windshield.

"What is it?"

"There is a trading post a little way ahead," the man replied, this being his explanation.

He climbed out of the Land Rover and walked ahead a little. He squatted suddenly and examined the ground, reaching out to touch the grass. After a moment he rose and moved forward again, then repeated the inspection of the ground. Rising, he turned and rejoined Bolan.

"Two men on foot came this way earlier this morning, men wearing military boots. They carried weapons, Belasko. I believe they could be waiting for us at the trading post."

Obotu watched Bolan's face. He chuckled softly to himself.

"What?" Bolan asked.

"It is true. The marks from the soles show in the dust. Deep marks because the men are carrying packs and weapons that make them heavier. They rested just ahead before they went to the post. One of them put his rifle against the ground when he stopped. The mark of the wooden stock can be seen. If they were local men, they would have bare feet. And if they had on footwear, it would not be this kind."

"Could be a couple of Mdofa's trackers."

Obotu nodded.

Keeping his tone conversational, Bolan said, "Are they skilled men?"

"Yes,"Obotu replied, a frown beginning to crease his face.

Bolan's hand closed over the AK-74 that lay beside him. He lifted it slowly and scanned the area.

"Then why have they left such clear tracks?"

Obotu's eyes widened in alarm, though he kept his composure, remaining still.

"Just walk to the rear and move fast when I give you the word," Bolan said.

Speaking in lighthearted tones, the African moved to the rear of the Land Rover, smiling as he spoke to McBride.

Bolan, watching through the side mirror, saw Obotu pause at the back of the Land Rover, his hand resting almost casually on the tailgate's top edge.

"Go!" Bolan yelled.

He saw the man grab the tailgate and begin to scramble over the top.

The Executioner's right foot slammed on the gas pedal, and his left eased off the clutch. The Land Rover surged forward, its engine roaring. The tires spun, raising clouds of dust, and the unwieldy vehicle rocked from side to side as it picked up speed.

Behind him Bolan could hear both Obotu and McBride yelling.

Then the stillness of the hot afternoon was shattered by a burst of autofire that sent streams of bullets at the Land Rover and its passengers.

21

The shots were coming from ahead of the Land Rover and off to the left. Bolan saw leaves being shredded in the thicket ahead where the hidden autorifle was being fired. Bullets struck the Land Rover's windshield; the toughened glass didn't break, it simply starred.

Behind him the Executioner heard other slugs thudding into the sides of the vehicle, and he quickly realized that it wasn't going to take long before someone was hit.

He plucked a grenade from his harness, pulled the pin with his teeth and lobbed the bomb into the thicket ahead of the vehicle. The detonation tossed a cloud of torn vegetation and earth into the air. It rained over the onrushing Land Rover, causing Bolan to swerve aside.

An African clad in camou gear stumbled into view, shaking his head to clear away the sound of the explosion.

The Executioner jammed the butt of the AK-74 against his hip, swiveling the barrel, and as he drove past the African he triggered a short burst that ripped into the man's chest and laid him flat on his back.

From the rear of the Land Rover came the boom of the SPAS combat shotgun, as McBride fired on the second ambusher. The rifle fell silent.

Bolan hauled on the wheel, bringing the Land Rover around in a tight circle, so that the vehicle was facing the way it had come.

He spotted the second attacker. The guy had dropped to his knees to avoid the shotgun blast. Now he scrambled to his feet, lifting his rifle to open fire. Bolan trod on the brake, springing from the seat as the vehicle shuddered to a halt. He shouldered the AK-74 and sighted briefly before laying down a volley that cut into the ambusher's body, stitching a bloody track down his torso to cut his legs from beneath him. The guy went down heavily, moaning in agony.

Bolan got to the gunner before the man could reach out and pick up his fallen rifle. The African stared up at the Executioner, his face registering the pain from his wounds. The Executioner's shots had damaged him badly, and blood was pulsing steadily from severed arteries.

"You need a doctor," Bolan said. "If you don't get help, you'll die soon."

The man grinned through his pain. "No doctor here. Not for a long way."

Obotu appeared at Bolan's side. He eyed the wounded man with open hostility, then turned to the Executioner.

"You see the kind of fools Mdofa has in his army. They believe he is Chandra's salvation. But Mdofa wants the country for himself. Not for anyone else. He is a pig who will take everything in the trough, and leave the rest starving."

The wounded African twisted his upper body as he tried to grab Obotu. The smaller man danced away, taunting him. The soldier fell back, struggling for breath through bloodied lips.

"Mdofa will never rule without the people behind him. And that will be never."

"You will see!" the wounded man raged despite his injuries. "Mdofa will bring us all to victory after Joffi dies tomorrow!"

"Tomorrow?" Bolan crouched by the man. "Where tomorrow?"

The soldier refused to say any more, realizing he had already given away too much. His outburst had weakened him, and he lay panting for breath.

"Give him to me, Belasko. I will make him talk," Obotu vowed.

"No, Matthias," McBride said from where she stood beside the Land Rover, "not that way."

The African rounded on her. "There are times for mercy and times for other things, McBride. This one knows something."

"If you make him tell you by torture, Matthias, you're no better than Mdofa. You come down to his level."

"Let's move out," Bolan said, standing. "It doesn't matter. He's dead."

THEY REACHED the main highway leading to the city just after dark. In the deepening gloom they could see the hazy lights in the distance, about five miles away.

Bolan gunned the Land Rover across the highway and rolled down a dusty slope. Obotu guided him along a rutted track and beneath a wooden trestle that carried the main railway tracks into the city. Bolan cut the engine.

"We need to find out where Joffi is, and we need to locate Mdofa and his forces. If something's going to happen tomorrow, it doesn't leave us much time."

"I can ask on the streets," Obotu suggested. "Information is available if you listen in the right places."

"First I want to get Kelly somewhere safe," Bolan said.

He was standing beside the Land Rover, staring up through the trestle to the railroad ties.

"How often do the trains run?" he asked.

Obotu stood beside him, a puzzled expression on his weathered face.

"I do not understand."

"By the time they reach here they should be slowing down."

"Yes, you're right, Belasko. But why is that of interest?"

"It would be a good chance for someone to get on board and ride into the city."

The African chuckled. "Yes."

Bolan shrugged out of the combat harness and got rid of the sheathed knife. He felt Obotu watching him.

The African was staring at the parang. Bolan picked it up again.

"You want it?"

Obotu nodded and took the weapon. He drew it from the sheath, smiling as he gazed at the gleaming, curved blade.

"Matthias, I could do with some civilian clothes. I'm not going to get far in the city dressed like this."

The African pondered for a few moments.

"I could trade some of the weapons for cash," he said. "Then I could buy clothes."

He took a pair of the AK-74s and four magazines. He rolled them up in one of the blankets from the back of the Land Rover.

Bolan, meanwhile, had emptied his pockets of the extra ammunition for the AK-74s. He kept the spare mag for the Desert Eagle and the heavy folding knife. He dumped the contents of the rucksack he'd brought along and packed the Franchi SPAS shotgun in the empty sack after reloading it. The barrel of the weapon stuck out of the top, so the warrior tore off a section from one of the blankets and wrapped it around the barrel. He collected all the spare shotgun cartridges and dropped them inside the sack, as well as the Browning Hi-Power that Kelly had been carrying.

"What about the rest of the weapons?" Obotu asked.

"If they're still here when you come back from the city," Bolan replied, "you can have them. Sell them to get more food for your village."

"In that case I will hide them."

Obotu spread the last blanket across the ground and quickly emptied the locker. Wrapping the weapons, he dragged the bundle away from the trestle and dug a shallow hole with the knife and his bare hands in the sandy earth. He rolled the blanket into the hole, covered it and expertly wiped away any signs.

Bolan took the opportunity to catch McBride's attention. "How do you feel about jumping a freight train?"

The woman grinned. "I'll try anything once."

THE LOCOMOTIVE PULLING the long line of freight cars threw out thick clouds of smoke from its stack. Steam hissed from loose valves. The train shuddered and clanked as the engineer applied the brakes, slowing as it reached the trestle. According to Obotu, this was the spot that marked the final approach to Chandra's capital. Ahead, on the fringes of the sprawling city, the rail lines merged in the untidy chaos of the freight yards.

Just beyond the trestle, crouching in the darkness beside the tracks, Bolan, McBride and Obotu waited for the opportune moment to board the crawling train.

As it rattled across the trestle, Bolan scanned the cars as they rolled by. There were open flatbed cars as well as boxcars. He spotted an oncoming boxcar that had its doors open.

"We'll take this one," he said.

As the boxcar drew level the warrior pushed to his feet, pulling McBride with him. He tossed the rucksack in through the door, then boosted McBride onto the floor of the car. Catching hold of the doorframe, Bolan pulled himself on board. Obotu, close behind, pushed his wrapped bundle before him, then scrambled in through the door.

As the warrior straightened, he heard a scrape of sound behind him. He turned and saw a huddled group of Africans pushing tightly into a corner of the car. They were dressed in ragged clothing, and wide eyes stared at him from gaunt faces.

Before Bolan could do anything, McBride stepped past him, speaking gently to the Africans. Her words seemed to have the desired effect, calming the frightened group. In a short time she was squatting on the floor, talking animatedly with them.

"People trust McBride," Obotu said. "She is a good person."

"Yeah," Bolan agreed. "You said it all, Matthias."

The Executioner leaned against the open doorframe, watching the lights of the city draw closer. Somewhere within the urban sprawl he had to find Lenard Mdofa and his coconspirators, including José Contreros.

22

Bolan stared at his reflection in the mirror that hung from a nail in the wall. He had just spent a painful ten minutes carefully shaving. Removing the growth of whiskers had exposed his bruised features. The African sun had burned his face a deep brown but not enough to hide all the marks from the beating he'd received at Mdofa's base.

He rinsed the lather from his face and toweled himself dry. For the first time in days he felt clean. The bathroom's ancient shower had sluiced away the dust and grime, easing some of the ache from his bones. Bolan ran his hands through his hair, wrapped a towel around his waist and returned to the bedroom.

He crossed the dimly lighted room and picked up the pile of clothes Matthias Obotu had brought. The African's eye had proved to be keener than any tailor's. His choice of clothing fit Bolan as if they had been made for him. Pulling on the shorts, the warrior picked up the dark blue, short-sleeved sport shirt and slipped it over his head, then put on the dark slacks and fastened the belt. Even the socks and shoes fit. Picking up the black windbreaker, Bolan dropped the spare magazine for the Desert Eagle into the zippered inner pocket.

He glanced at his watch, now set to local time, and saw that it was coming up to 8:45. Obotu had promised to be back before nine, with any news he had managed to pick up on the city streets.

They had been in the capital for a couple of hours. From the freight yard Obotu had guided them through the expanding refugee camps and shantytowns ringing the city, and had brought them to this crumbling hotel in the heart of the old quarter.

During the days of British rule, the Royal Hotel had been *the* place to stay. Things had changed since independence. Luxury, as provided by the Royal, fell out of favor, and the establishment's fortunes changed. Now it provided cheap accommodation without the frills. There was no telephone in Bolan's room, or television. The cheap plastic radio wasn't working, and the plumbing had turned out to be erratic. McBride's room, down the hall, was identical in its lack of amenities.

One thing it did offer was anonymity. Obotu had obtained rooms without any problem. The man behind the desk was a distant relative. He had barely taken any notice of Bolan and McBride.

Once they were established in the rooms, Obotu vanished with his wrapped bundle of AK-74s. He had been back within the hour, carrying parcels that had contained clothing for both Bolan and Kelly. The African had left almost immediately, eager to return to the streets, where he said he had already picked up rumors about possible trouble that would occur the next day.

Bolan was starting to worry. He wanted Obotu back safely. The longer the African was on the streets asking questions, the greater the chance he might attract the wrong kind of attention.

Standing by the window, the Executioner looked out across the city. Somewhere, cloaked by the night, were the shadowy figures Bolan needed to find. Darkness was the conspirators' friend and ally. They performed their evil better under the mantle of night, hidden away, their intentions expressed in hushed whispers, out of sight and out of earshot.

The Executioner's desire was to drag them into the sunlight, to expose them in the bright glare of day. But he needed a direction, a point of reference.

Matthias Obotu was his guide.

Beyond the old quarter the modern city of Charaville blazed with light. Despite the internal problems plaguing the country, President Joffi was working to improve its image. He was bringing in outside investors, trying to create employment with a building program. Housing and industry were two of his main projects. Aware of the country's need for food and water, Joffi had recently been encouraging new ways to promote farming. There had been small returns but not enough to feed a starving nation. Until the drought ended, Chandra's main problem was going to remain. Only the unstinting aid provided by organizations such as the Piet Sonderstrom Aid Group, importing food and medical supplies, kept things going. But even that was only providing a tiny percentage of the nation's need.

The situation was fuel for Lenard Mdofa's inflammatory harangues against the government. He used the deep-rooted problems to bolster his case for reform. Only Mdofa, like his brother dictators, always managed to avoid explaining exactly how he would perform any better than the elected government. He didn't explain because he couldn't. The man had no policy. He simply wanted to turn the populace against the government so his takeover could happen during a time of unrest, when the government had its hands full trying to quell the demands of a suffering majority. By the time realization came, Mdofa would be in control and his terror squads would show his true colors.

Unless they were stopped.

A knock on the door pulled Bolan away from the window.

"Mike, it's me."

Bolan opened the door, and McBride stepped into the room, dressed in light slacks and a cool blouse. Her hair had been brushed until it shone. Only her face, red from exposure, showed she had been through hard times.

"How are you feeling?" he asked.

"Fine. Mike, I have to get to the directors of our local office. There are things I have to discuss with them. It's time they were made aware of what's been going on."

"You sure that's wise?"

"I know what you're going to say, but this is my part of the war. Remember what you said about making decisions and carrying them through? I'm doing just that. I won't allow Mdofa to scare me off."

"Well, you're scaring me," Bolan said. "I feel sorry for anyone who gets in the way."

"That cargo of containers we left in Rotterdam could be on its way here. For all we know those weapons could be included. They have to be stopped from getting any farther than the docks."

"That cargo ship won't be here for days, Kelly. Why not wait?"

She shook her head. "No, Mike. I'm not standing by any longer. This has to be faced. My friends are involved. They have a right to know what's been happening."

Bolan realized the woman wouldn't be swayed. He crossed the room and removed the Browning from its hiding place.

"You want to take this with you?"

She smiled. "I'll leave that part to you, Mike. From past experience I'm sure you'll have a use for it."

"How will you get there?"

"I went downstairs and had the desk clerk order me a taxi. Don't worry. I'll be fine. I know the city well, and I know the people."

"Be careful, Kelly. Mdofa is still free and clear at the moment."

The woman leaned forward and kissed him. "Later," she said.

He moved to the window after she had left and watched her step into the taxi that pulled up at the curb. Then she was gone.

Ten minutes later a car slid to a hasty stop outside. Bolan saw Matthias Obotu hurry from the vehicle and into the hotel. There was an urgency in the little African's movements that warned Bolan things were not well.

The warrior tucked the Browning under his belt in the small of his back. The Desert Eagle went at the side of his waistband. He pulled on a windbreaker and bent to pick up the SPAS shotgun.

The door opened and Obotu stood there, sweating and looking scared.

"Problems?" Bolan asked.

"I think your expression would be that I've blown it."

"What have you found out?"

"Too much, I think."

Bolan grabbed the rucksack containing the extra shells for the SPAS. They quit the room and went down the stairs. Crossing the lobby, they reached the parked car, a battered and much-abused Oldsmobile that looked to be at least twenty years old.

"I borrowed it from a friend," Obotu explained. He took the rucksack from Bolan and threw it through the open rear window onto the back seat.

The howl of sliding tires announced the arrival of company. Bolan glanced over his shoulder and saw a gleaming black Mercedes hurtling toward them. There was no mistaking the intent.

Obotu ran around the front of the car, pulling open the driver's door despite Bolan's warning to stay back.

The Mercedes bore down on them with frightening speed. A figure leaned out the rear passenger door and leveled a stubby autoweapon.

"Matthias!"

Bolan's yell was drowned out by the stuttering burst of gunfire.

There was a stunned groan from the African as his body caught the brunt of the volley, then he was slammed back against the part-open door.

The Executioner raced around the rear of the Oldsmobile, shaking off the blanket that covered the SPAS combat shotgun. When he reached the middle of the street, he swept up the shotgun to hip level. Turning the black muzzle on the rear of the Mercedes as it powered away, Bolan triggered the full 7-shot load, riding the kick of the powerful weapon.

He saw the rear window burst apart, heard the clang as shot ripped into the trunk. A rear tire blew, the steel rim of the wheel burning sparks as it hit the street. The Mercedes swerved, bucking as the driver trod on the brake. The vehicle lurched, then came to a faltering stop. The rear end flashed fire as the ruptured tank spilled gasoline onto the hot exhaust and it ignited, sending a column of flame and smoke into the night sky. Doors on the vehicle burst open, and armed hardmen spilled wildly onto the street. At least one of them went down from wounds already sustained from Bolan's shotgun attack.

The warrior dropped the SPAS to the street and pulled the Desert Eagle. He brought the big autopistol up in a two-handed grip, leveling and firing in a fluid action. His first shot took out the lead gunner, planting a slug in his chest and knocking him over on his back. Ignoring the frantic bursts of autofire coming his way, Bolan tracked and fired with cool efficiency, each shot counting. He dropped all three hardmen, taking out the final one with a pair of shots to the left leg. The guy pitched facedown on the street, screaming in agony, clamping his hands around the pulped ruin of his thigh.

When he reached the man, Bolan flipped him over on his back and thrust the hot muzzle of the Desert Eagle into the guy's screwed up, pasty-white face.

"You've got about five seconds before I pull this trigger, pal," Bolan warned, "so come up with the right answers."

The merc stared fixedly at the shards of bone protruding from his leg and decided to cut his losses before it was too late.

"Okay, okay. Redland sent us. Your African buddy has been all over town asking questions. One of our people learned how he'd come in with a red-haired woman and a big white guy. Hell, it didn't take much to figure it was you."

He moaned as pain flared.

Bolan put some pressure on the Desert Eagle, digging it into the merc's flesh.

"So where are they?"

"Mdofa's place outside of town. Big house in its own grounds. You can't get in. He's got it sewn up tighter than a drum, and he's about the same. Belasko, you got under his skin. That guy is really pissed. He won't come out of there."

"Until tomorrow?" Bolan asked, watching for any reaction.

Surprise showed in the merc's eyes.

"How in hell did you..."

"It's not your concern."

The burning Mercedes blew again with a hollow thump, the rear end lifting as flame blossomed.

Beyond the noise, Bolan heard the distant whine of sirens. He climbed to his feet and retraced his steps to the Oldsmobile, snatching up the SPAS. When he reached the car, he saw that Obotu was behind the wheel. There was blood on the street and the inside of the door. The little African already had the engine running.

"Get in quickly, Belasko," he said through bloody lips.

Bolan ran around to the passenger side and climbed in. Obotu gunned the engine and the Oldsmobile took off with a screech of tires. Its performance belied its age.

"My friend has a special touch with engines," Obotu explained.

The Executioner reached for the rucksack, took out a handful of cartridges for the shotgun and began to reload.

"How bad are you hurt?" Bolan asked.

He had already seen the glistening mass of blood down the African's front. Now it was soaking his pants.

"It is more than a scratch."

Obotu took them away from the hotel area via a succession of narrow back streets and alleys.

"Do you know where Mdofa's residence is? The one outside town?"

Obotu nodded. "I can get you there."

He pushed the speeding car across an intersection, ignoring the blare of horns from other vehicles.

"Mdofa is frightened. You have interfered with his plans and forced his hand. His people have been scouring the city looking for you. By the time I realized just how many there were, it was too late. Belasko, you are a marked man. I came back to warn you."

The car swerved as Obotu almost lost control. With an effort he pulled it straight again.

"I have learned that Joffi is to make a public appearance tomorrow to open a new wing at the city hospital. It would be the obvious choice for Mdofa."

Bolan racked in the last shell, completing the reloading of the SPAS, and stuffed the remaining cartridges into his pocket. After ejecting the near-spent clip for the Desert Eagle, he snapped in his last magazine.

The city fell away around them as Obotu pushed the Oldsmobile through a residential area. Gradually the properties began to space out. The ones they were passing now were walled off, the distances between them greater. Soon they were rolling along an asphalt road bounded on one side by forested plains and undulating terrain on the other. Bolan could taste the salty tang in the air that rushed through the open window of the car.

"We are on the coast here," Obotu explained. "Mdofa's residence lies on a bay looking out to sea.

He has his own mooring facility and even a landing place for helicopters. It used to belong to a wealthy French businessman many years ago."

Fifteen minutes later the African pulled the car around a bend in the road, braking quickly. A side road led off the main highway, down a slight incline to high gates blocking off the entrance to Lenard Mdofa's imposing residence. Walls circled the grounds. The main building was sprawling and one-level, gleaming a dull white under the sullen night sky. The house was encompassed by a mass of cultivated gardens, complete with fountains and ornamental pools. At the rear a wide patio area reached as far as the extreme edge of the property. Steps led down to the water that lapped at the base of the slope below the residence. Over on the far right Bolan made out the illuminated helipad and the dark bulk of Mdofa's Hind gunship.

Obotu leaned his head on the steering wheel. His breathing was shallow, accompanied by moist wheezing. He sat motionless, his slender body trembling in response to the pain coursing through him. The seat where he sat was slick with blood.

"Matthias," Bolan said gently.

"You cannot help me, Belasko. Your business lies below. Mdofa must not kill Joffi. His evil must be stopped. Do that for me and I will rest in peace."

Bolan stepped out of the car, the SPAS tucked under his arm. He stepped to the edge of the road and scanned the area.

It was a tight spot to break into.

Behind him the Oldsmobile rumbled gently as Obotu teased the gas pedal. Bolan heard the tires crunch over stones as the African allowed the car to roll forward, catching up to him.

"Belasko," Obotu said as he drew level with the tall American, "you are wondering how to get inside?"

"It crossed my mind."

The African smiled wearily.

"That is easy. I can open a way for you."

Realization struck Bolan in the same instant Obotu jammed his foot hard on the gas pedal. The highly tuned Oldsmobile roared, tires smoking as it lurched forward, picking up speed. The incline helped to build the big vehicle's momentum. By the time it hit the gates it was doing more than fifty. There was a screech of tortured metal as the heavy Olds ripped through the gates, taking down most of one stone pillar in the process. It hurtled across the parking area inside the gates, slewing to one side just before it smashed into the expensive Mercedes sedan parked near the entrance to the house itself. Locked together by the impact, the two cars slid into the front wall of the building, demolishing part of it and shattering a large picture window. Burst pipes that fed the ornaments around the garden spewed water into the air, and torn electric cables from the many lights sparked and crackled, adding to the confusion.

Mack Bolan, unable to stop Matthias Obotu from carrying out his reckless action, saw that the African was presenting him with an opportunity to gain entry to Mdofa's stronghold.

The Executioner broke into a run, following the car down the side road, determined not to allow Matthias to make an empty gesture.

As the car hit the gates and vanished from sight, Bolan threw himself forward and flattened against the the outer wall, mere feet from the breached entrance.

He held his position for no more than a few seconds, giving Matthias's appearance time to register on those inside. Then he gained his feet and sprinted for the entrance, wondering just what he might face once he was inside.

23

Bolan ducked into the shadows just beyond the breached gates. He slipped in among dense shrubbery, crouching when he heard a shout, followed by the chatter of an autoweapon. The burst was long, and as it ended, Bolan could hear the sharp ring of shell casings striking the stone slabs as they were ejected from the rapid-fire weapon.

"Only one of them, goddamn it!" someone yelled.

"Belasko must be near! Find him! I want him dead! A bonus to the man who brings me his head!"

Bolan easily recognized the high-pitched tones of Lenard Mdofa. He pushed deeper into the shrubbery, eyes and ears alert.

He picked up the light footfall to his left and turned quickly, almost colliding with the uniformed guard. The African reacted fast, swinging up his AK-74, finger beginning to curl around the trigger. Bolan had already initiated his move, and he drove the heavy SPAS shotgun into the guard's stomach. The guy choked, bending forward, and caught the solid bulk of the SPAS across the back of his neck. Something snapped, and the guy flattened on the ground, loose-limbed and face-first.

Bolan picked up the dropped AK-74 and slung it over his shoulder by the strap. As the movement of Mdofa's guards began to build up, the warrior melted farther into the darkness of the expansive gardens, circling away from the gates.

His combat senses, honed by years of similar situations, allowed him to spot his targets well before they were aware of him.

The Executioner's first strike was against a pair of guards, thrusting their way into the foliage, using the barrels of their rifles to part the greenery. Their only indication of the warrior's move was a split-second glimpse of a dark figure rising in front of them. Then the night exploded in their faces as Bolan triggered two fast shots from the SPAS. The shredded corpses crashed to the ground, leaving a trail of blood-spattered shrubbery in their wake. By the time the bodies were found, Bolan had slipped away, moving again, circling silently.

He brushed against the perimeter wall, pausing briefly to replace the two cartridges before crouching and peering through the shadows to where another armed hardman stood revealed by the pale glow of lamplight behind him.

The combat shotgun rose, was leveled and fired. The outlined figure seemed to burst apart, crashing to the ground with a rustle of foliage.

This time Bolan held his ground and took out another of Mdofa's guards as the man came to investigate his dead companion's fate.

"Move out, damn it, he's only one man! Push him into the open!"

Flat on the ground, his lean form eased beneath the overhanging shrubbery, Bolan watched the running feet of searching men pass him by. This time he held his fire and retreated for a distance, then changed his direction and pushed forward again, using the natural cover of the lush garden and its overabundant vegetation.

Pressed close against the curving trunk of a massive tree, Bolan exchanged weapons. He braced the butt of the AK-74 against his shoulder, sighted down the barrel and tracked one of Mdofa's white mercenaries as the man peered inside the wrecked Oldsmobile. The warrior's finger stroked the trigger and sent a single 5.45 mm hollowpoint winging its way to impact with the merc's head. The tumbling effect of the bullet cored a massive trough through the hardman's skull, and he was dead before he hit the ground.

A second man burst into sight, firing wildly, his autoweapon sending a stream of slugs in Bolan's general direction. The man had failed to pinpoint his target so he was simply saturating the area, hoping to force Bolan into the open. His strategy might have been sound, but the desired result failed to materialize.

The warrior had eased around to the far side of the thick trunk and he took out the gunman with a single shot that kicked the guy off his feet and dumped him on the ground in a bloody heap.

Snatching up the SPAS, Bolan doubled back the way he'd come, slinging the AK-74 over his shoulder again. Coming around a thick stand of flowering bushes, he came across a trio of guards. They opened fire, crisscrossing the area. Bolan had instinctively dropped groundward, below the fusillade.

As fast as he was, one of the slugs caught him in the left side, just above the hip. It created a shallow wound, tearing flesh and spilling blood. Bolan hit the ground a fraction of a second later, too involved in the heat of the moment to concern himself about the wound. He was already bringing the barrel of the shotgun to bear on the three men. His finger worked the SPAS's trigger, emptying the entire load of shells into the trio, turning living men into shuddering, torn shapes that spilled to the ground in a welter of bloody flesh.

Pushing to his feet, the warrior tossed aside the empty shotgun. His supply of cartridges was used up. He brought the AK-74 into play again, melting into the depths of the garden once more, cutting back and forth between shadows and foliage as he stalked the searching force employed to protect Lenard Mdofa.

In the darkness of the gardens that had suddenly become a part of hell, the members of Mdofa's elite became the hunted. The cultivated earth, carefully watered and fed to maintain Mdofa's sprawling land-scaped gardens, became littered with the corpses of his dream. Blood and death dominated that place, leaving no doubt as to who had the upper hand.

The Executioner picked them off singly now, pushing his advantage, refusing to slacken his killing pace. He was tracking his main quarry, taking out the troops on the way. He gave them no respite. If they challenged him, they died. If they threw aside their weapons and crept away in the darkness, he let them go.

His objective was the house itself, where the top men could be waiting.

Bolan eased past the wrecked Oldsmobile, pausing to pick up a discarded AK-74 and eject the magazine. Crouching beside the car, eyes and ears searching for any danger, the warrior replaced his near-exhausted magazine for the fresh one.

In the brief seconds he paused beside the car, he peered in through the buckled driver's door. Matthias Obotu lay twisted and bloody across the seat, his body further riddled by autofire, one more innocent cut down for daring to oppose Mdofa.

The area lay silent and still.

Bolan moved around to the far side of the Oldsmobile, then used the wrecked Mercedes as cover. Stepping over crumbling masonry and broken glass, he slipped quietly into the house through the shattered picture window. The warrior flattened against the wall and checked out the room he was in, noting the expensive furniture and decor. At the far end two steps led up to the double doors that stood open. Light shone from the room beyond. Bolan cat-footed to the doors, paused again and slid down to a crouch before peering around the doorframe.

A large, open reception area lay before him. The floor was smooth, polished natural wood. The painted walls were decorated with tribal objets d'art. Directly across from Bolan was a wide stone archway leading deeper into the house.

The Executioner remained where he was. His patience was rewarded when he heard the merest creak of shoe leather coming from his right. Someone lay in wait, out of his field of vision, most probably hugging the wall near the main entrance.

Crouching there, Bolan felt a sudden swell of pain from the bullet tear in his side. He had forgotten about it during the time he'd spent outside. Now that he'd been still for a short while, the pain was making itself known. Looking down, he saw that a large wet bloodstain had soaked through his shirt. He pushed the discomfort to the back of his mind. He would worry about the wound later.

He listened for any other sounds from the reception area. Nothing reached his ears. He braced himself, then lunged up and out, taking a long dive across the polished floor. Bolan landed on his shoulder, rolling a couple of times before coming to rest on his front. He turned his upper body and pushed out the AK-74, searching for his target.

And found it.

A single gunner turned his 9 mm Uzi in Bolan's direction, trying to make up for the initial loss of his target. His Uzi chattered loudly, throwing a stream of slugs at the warrior. Splinters exploded from the wood floor, advancing as the gunner corrected his aim.

Bolan held his fire for a second longer, making certain he had target acquisition before he triggered a trio of shots.

The slugs drilled the gunner in the chest, spinning him backward. He slumped against the wall and bounced off, throwing his arms wide in panic. For a scant second he was motionless. Then he toppled backward and crashed through the glass panel that stood beside the main entrance doors.

The Executioner got to his feet and trotted across the reception area and through the archway. The wall on his left was made entirely of a long window. Beyond lay the wide patio, brightly floodlit, and, farther on, well clear of the house, was the helipad. The Hind gunship's rotors were slowly turning.

Bolan picked out the running figures of Lenard Mdofa and José Contreros.

The rats were deserting the sinking ship.

But where was Redland?

A distorted image flickered in the glass behind the reflection of Bolan's own figure.

The Executioner moved to one side an instant before the flashing blade of a heavy knife could bury itself between his shoulders. He kept on moving, turning his body, and caught a glimpse of an angry, taut face behind the lethal blade.

Liam Redland.

The merc snatched a quick breath, bracing himself for another thrust, his reflexes swift and sure.

Bolan blocked with the assault rifle, catching the blade against the metal barrel. He twisted the rifle, forcing the knife down. The action pulled Redland closer to the warrior. With a sudden reversal of direction, Bolan slammed his right shoulder into Redland's face. It caught the merc across the jaw and rocked his head back.

The warrior swept the AK-74 around in a brutal arc that cracked against the bridge of Redland's nose. Bone crunched and the merc staggered away, blood gushing from his nose. Bolan kept pace with him, the assault rifle sweeping from left to right, thudding into the merc's body until he fell back against the wall. He slithered to the floor, still clutching the knife, until Bolan stepped on his wrist and put his full weight on it. Redland's fingers opened and the knife slipped free. Bolan reached down and picked up the knife, turning almost casually. Redland's eyes caught those of the Executioner, and then Liam Redland realized who he had been up against. In a desperate move he lunged up off the floor, his outstretched hands going for the warrior's throat.

It was no contest. Bolan's right hand made a swift, deep cut across Redland's throat. The merc gave a startled gasp that was lost in the rush of blood from his severed flesh. His limbs twitched violently as he slumped to one side, then rolled slowly until one side of his face was pressed awkwardly against the smooth, polished wood of the floor. An expanding pool of blood began to creep out from under his head.

The Executioner moved on until he reached the doors that allowed him to step outside. He crossed the wide, elaborate patio, with its expensive pieces of sculpture and potted plants. He could hear the building whine of the Hind's powerful engines.

Mdofa and Contreros had almost reached the big chopper when Bolan raised the assault rifle and sighted along its barrel.

He fired a single shot and José Contreros stumbled, regained his balance, then fell to his knees. The warrior adjusted his aim and fired again. The Colombian jerked forward as if someone had pulled a string. He fell facedown, hard, his body shuddering. Contreros had cut his last deal.

Mdofa had one foot on the step and was about to pull himself up into the hatchway of the Hind. He glanced in Bolan's direction, then snatched at the SIG-Sauer holstered on his hip.

The AK-74 bucked in Bolan's hands, each shot followed by another until the clip ran dry. Mdofa's lean body, clad in its immaculate uniform and gleaming boots, was torn apart by the stream of slugs. The expanding projectiles ravaged the would-be dictator's flesh, extinguishing his life and ending his ambitious scheme to wrest power from the legal head of state and initiate his personal brand of terror on a suffering nation. His lifeless corpse dropped from the step and onto the concrete.

Bolan threw down the empty rifle and drew the Desert Eagle. He pressed his left hand over the aching wound in his side and turned back to the house. He was looking for a telephone. With a little luck he might be able to get a call through to Brognola at the Farm. There was a need now for some diplomatic help. Someone in Washington was going to have to call President Victor Joffi and let him know just what had been going on behind his back. It might help to take some of the heat off Mack Bolan, because very soon it was going to come down on the Executioner with a vengeance. There would be some frantic discussions and some red faces before it was all tidied up. But as far as the Executioner was concerned, the political manipulators could sort that out.

The mission was over, and all accounts were settled.

EPILOGUE

"It's going to take weeks to sort out the paperwork," Brognola admitted. "The President wants a minute-by-minute report on the whole affair."

Mack Bolan smiled as he listened to the big Fed's grumbling over the telephone.

"You'll handle it," he said. "All I want now is an update."

"The British police picked up Evan Brewer when he tried to sneak back into England. They're holding him so that our people can ask him questions."

"Van Hooten?"

"He decided to go the hard way when the Dutch police went to arrest him. Tried to shoot it out with them and ended up dead. They found information in his apartment that incriminated a couple of customs officers. These were the guys who faked the manifests for the containers carrying weapons. Altered the weight records and passed them as okay."

"The drug dealers?"

"All quiet at the moment. They'll fade into the background for a while, but they'll be back. Your blitz has left them thin on the ground."

"Small gains."

"On the downside, Striker, the Dutch police found Charlie Diel's body in one of the canals. Somebody had given him a hard time before they killed him."

Bolan sighed. It was always the good ones who were made to die badly.

"Your visit to Chandra stirred up some dust," Brognola finally said. "President Joffi was mad as hell until our people over there showed him the documentary evidence left by Mdofa. It made Joffi take a long, hard look at his own administration. He even made a personal visit to Mdofa's base and saw for himself what had been going on. After that he came down hard on his people. Had quite a pile of resignations on his desk the next day."

"He was lucky this time," Bolan said. "Mdofa might have succeeded if Diel's undercover work hadn't made the connection."

"I think Joffi got the message, Striker. Especially when he took a look at the video his security people shot after they were flown out to the ship to film that opened-up medical container. Unofficially he's expressed his appreciation."

Bolan made no reply to that. He wasn't standing in line for thanks. Medals didn't rate very highly when they were lined up against suffering and death. People were what mattered, not plaudits.

"So how are the Greek Islands?"

"Bearable."

"It was decided that getting you out of Chandra was the diplomatic thing to do."

"Seeing as how I didn't volunteer to go there in the first place," Bolan reminded him.

"I thought you were still in Holland. Our people were scouring the country, and all the while you were in Africa."

"Yeah."

"How's the lady taking it?"

"She's calmed down now."

"She can go back in a couple of weeks. The Sonderstrom organization has tightened up its own security. They've linked up with another freight company now that the police have closed down Star Freight. It's surprising what the police found when they went in. Contraband should have been Star's middle name, from what I heard they were into—porn, drugs, money laundering. They'd ship anything, anywhere."

Bolan stared out across the balcony of the hotel room at blue sky and sea. Distant sounds rose up from the beach—the noise and chatter of people enjoying themselves, children shrieking and laughing as they played. It was a world far removed from the horrors of Chandra where drought and famine, coupled with sudden death, seemed to be the norm.

He heard the soft pad of bare feet behind him and picked up the gentle drift of perfume. Kelly McBride appeared beside him.

"Striker, you still there?" Brognola asked.

Bolan put the receiver to his ear again.

"Still here."

"Anything else we need to cover?"

McBride looked expectant and showed signs of impatience.

"One thing," Bolan said.

"Yeah?"

"Next time you figure I need some R & R, let's discuss it first. Looks to me like we have different points of view on what constitutes R & R."

Brognola cleared his throat. "I guess I was wrong about Amsterdam, pal."

"A little," Bolan agreed. "Right now I'm on my own R & R. We'll talk."

Bolan hung up and took Kelly by the hand. Another mission was looming—of that he had no doubt. But now, just for a little while, the warrior decided to sample a few of life's pleasures. Tomorrow was another day.

America is the prime target in a global holocaust

STONY MAN™ 14

DEADLY AGENT

Joseph Ryba is the man who would be king—of a new
Bohemian empire. The Czech official is poised to unleash
a plague that would put Europe at his mercy. Germ warfare
missiles hidden stateside would render the world's watchdog
powerless. Mack Bolan, Able Team and Phoenix Force race
along a tightrope to find and dismantle the deadly arsenal
without forcing Ryba's hand—a situation that would result
in nothing short of global holocaust.

Take
4 explosive books
plus a
mystery bonus
FREE

Mail to: Gold Eagle Reader Service
          3010 Walden Ave.
          P.O. Box 1394
          Buffalo, NY 14240-1394

YEAH! Rush me 4 FREE Gold Eagle novels and my FREE mystery gift.
Then send me 4 brand-new novels every other month as they come off
the presses. Bill me at the low price of just $14.80* for each shipment—
a saving of 12% off the cover prices for all four books! There is NO extra
charge for postage and handling! There is no minimum number of books I
must buy. I can always cancel at any time simply by returning a shipment
at your cost or by returning any shipping statement marked "cancel." Even
if I never buy another book from Gold Eagle, the 4 free books and surprise
gift are mine to keep forever.

164 BPM ANQY

Name	(PLEASE PRINT)	
Address		Apt. No.
City	State	Zip

Signature (if under 18, parent or guardian must sign)

* Terms and prices subject to change without notice. Sales tax applicable in
  NY. This offer is limited to one order per household and not valid to
  present subscribers. Offer not available in Canada.

AC-94

When all is lost, there is
always the future

JAMES AXLER

DEATH LANDS®

Genesis Echo

The warrior survivalists are guests in a reactivated twentieth-century medical institute in Maine, where mad scientists pursue their abstract theories, oblivious to the realities of the world. When they take an unhealthy interest in Krysty Wroth, the pressure is on to find a way out of this guarded enclave.

In the Deathlands, the war for domination is over, but the struggle for survival continues.

**Don't miss out on the action in these titles featuring
THE EXECUTIONER®, ABLE TEAM® and PHOENIX FORCE®!**

SuperBolan

#61435   DEATH'S HEAD $4.99   ☐
            While in Berlin on a Mafia search-and-destroy, Bolan uncovers a covert
            cadre of ex-Soviets working with German neo-Nazis and other right-wing
            nationalists.

#61436   HELLGROUND $4.99   ☐
            In this business, you get what you pay for. Iberra's tab is running high—and
            the Executioner has come to collect.

Stony Man™

#61893   STONY MAN #9 STRIKEPOINT $4.99   ☐
            Free-lance talent from the crumbling Russian empire fuels Iraq's nuclear
            power.

#61894   STONY MAN #10 SECRET ARSENAL $4.99   ☐
            A biochemical weapons conspiracy puts America in the hot seat.

#61895   STONY MAN #11 TARGET AMERICA $4.99   ☐
            A terrorist strike calls America's top commandos to the firing line.

(limited quantities available on certain titles)

TOTAL AMOUNT	$	
POSTAGE & HANDLING	$	
($1.00 for one book, 50¢ for each additional)		
APPLICABLE TAXES*	$	_____
TOTAL PAYABLE	$	_____
(check or money order—please do not send cash)		

To order, complete this form and send it, along with a check or money order for
the total above, payable to Gold Eagle Books, to: **In the U.S.:** 3010 Walden Avenue,
P.O. Box 9077, Buffalo, NY 14269-9077; **In Canada:** P.O. Box 636, Fort Erie, Ontario,
L2A 5X3.

Name:_____

Address:_____ City:_____

State/Prov.:_____ Zip/Postal Code: _____

*New York residents remit applicable sales taxes.
 Canadian residents remit applicable GST and provincial taxes.